THE WATCHERS

ALSO BY BRADLEY BOOTH

Adventures in Galilee
Chains in China
Dare to Stand Alone
Escape From Egypt
Esther: A Star Is Born
Every Day With Jesus
Miracles of the Mantle
Miracle on the Mountain
Noah: The Chosen One
Noah: The End of the World
Plagues in the Palace
Prince of Dreams
The Prodigal
The Seventh-day Ox and Other Miracle Stories From Russia
Shepherd Warrior
Showers of Grasshoppers and Other Miracle Stories From Africa
They Call Him the Miracle Man
Time Warp

THE LOST TREASURES SERIES

Guardians of the Mercy Seat, book 1
The Watchers, book 2

THE LOST TREASURES SERIES

BRADLEY BOOTH

THE WATCHERS

Pacific Press®
Publishing Association

Nampa, Idaho | Oshawa, Ontario, Canada
www.pacificpress.com

Cover design by Gerald Lee Monks
Cover design resources by Marcus Mashburn

Copyright © 2017 by Pacific Press® Publishing Association
Printed in the United States of America

The author assumes full responsibility for the accuracy of all facts and quotations as cited in this book.

Additional copies of this book are available by calling toll-free 1-800-765-6955 or by visiting www.AdventistBookCenter.com.

ISBN: 978-0-8163-6278-3

February 2017

Dedication

This book is dedicated to God's faithful ones down through the ages who have watched and waited for the chance to honor His holy name.

1

Caleb sprinted up a mud-brick staircase inside the city wall. The hot afternoon breezes ruffled his thatch of jet-black hair as he reached the top of the stone steps. He stopped to catch his breath but jumped back suddenly as a military chariot raced past. "Get out of the way, kid!" the officer roared as the chariot sped away. "Wanna get hit?"

The boy's heart jumped into his throat at the near miss. The outer walls of Babylon were wide enough for three chariots to race side by side, but foot traffic always took second place to military chariots on the wall.

"There you are!" a wiry, dark-haired boy exclaimed as he caught sight of Caleb and ran to meet him. "It's about time you showed up. Where have you been?"

It was Tamzi, Caleb's friend who lived near the Jewish settlement in Babylon. At thirteen, he was a year younger than Caleb, but the two boys were the best of friends, even if they were from two very different cultures. Tamzi was a Babylonian, and his father worked for the governor as a curator in the royal archives.

Caleb ignored the scolding. "Yeah, yeah. My aunt Helah sent me to the market to get some things for the upcoming feast."

Caleb had many Jewish friends. Most of them were his cousins or boys he went to school with, but he enjoyed spending time with Tamzi as much as with any of them.

Tamzi knew about all the exciting things going on in Babylon, yet he wasn't a know-it-all, unlike Caleb's cousins Etam, Naam, and Zanoah. All they did was brag about how important their fathers were.

Tamzi and his family were good people, though they did have some strange beliefs about the gods of wood and stone they worshiped. They also ate some things Caleb would never even touch, such as pigs and sharks and mice.

Caleb was a Jew from the tribe of Judah and lived in the Jewish Quarter, which was south of the fish gate overlooking the Euphrates River. He was an orphan and had no recollection of his mother. He had been only two when she died while giving birth to his baby sister, Saarah. Then tragically, when he was four, his father had died as an officer in the Babylonian army.

Thankfully, he now lived with his aunt and uncle. Uncle Jabez was a kind man, just forty-two years of age. He was a hard worker and a real leader in the community. Aunt Helah, a pretty woman with dark hair, was a few years younger than Uncle Jabez and very supportive of her husband and their family pottery business. The couple had grown sons but loved Caleb and his sister as if they were their own children.

"Come on!" Tamzi gave Caleb's arm an impatient jerk. "My brother has news about the Medo-Persian army." The two boys raced to the nearest guard tower along the wall and arrived out of breath, with Caleb in the lead.

"Well, little Brother, you're going to have to eat more bread if you want to keep up with Caleb," Tamzi's brother, Isi, teased as he gave Tamzi a playful punch in the shoulder. Isi was a sentry in the forty-third guard tower on the western wall of Babylon. As far as Caleb was concerned, he was the best source of news when the two boys wanted to know anything about the army.

"Our scouts tell us the Medo-Persian army is on the march again," Isi said as he glanced out across the Plain of Dura. "Cyrus has conquered Media and Lydia, and some say he will come for Babylon next."

Tamzi's eyes narrowed to slits in the late afternoon sun. "Do you think they will conquer Babylon too?" he asked.

"Oh, probably not," Isi grinned. "They will have an awfully hard time.

Starving us out won't work. I'm told we've got enough food in the city to last twenty years." He gave Tamzi's head a playful rub. "And breaking through our walls is impossible. Look, let me show you." Isi stepped out of the guard tower. "See the wall here? It is actually two separate walls with sand piled between them. The sand won't let a battering ram break through the walls. Walls have to have empty spaces behind them for a battering ram to work."

Tamzi breathed a sigh of relief. "I hope you're right about that, but they say no one has stopped Cyrus yet. Everywhere he goes, he wins."

"Relax, little Brother." Isi held out his spear to Tamzi. "Here? Wanna help?"

Tamzi snatched the spear out of Isi's hand. "Very funny." Then he got a fierce look in his eye. "Just tell me where they are. I'll fight 'em!" he growled playfully.

"Yeah, right," Caleb grinned. "Let me know when that's going to happen. I want a front-row seat." He hopped down from the brick wall where he was sitting. "I've got to go home and do my chores," he said. "Can you come by later, Tamzi? If I get my work done, maybe we can go fishing."

"Sure," Tamzi grinned. "I can help with the chores if you need me. I'll do anything to go fishing."

Caleb hurried down the stairs to the street below. Shimmering heat rose from the brick streets of Babylon, and little gray lizards skittered left and right to get out of his way. As he hurried through the marketplace, he had to duck under a roll of carpet that was being hoisted onto the shoulder of a passing vendor. He sidestepped a camel loaded high with market goods, stumbled over a willowy basket of citrus in his pathway, and then hastily clutched at the doorpost of a merchant's stall. No matter. It was the only way to avoid being pushed aside by a squadron of Babylonian soldiers on their way somewhere.

He turned onto the street where he lived and entered the gate to the family courtyard. The family dwelling wasn't extravagant, but it wasn't shabby either. Doorways opened off the central courtyard into a kitchen area for preparing food, a workshop for making pottery, storage rooms, and stables for two donkeys and half a dozen milk goats. A stairway led to an upper level with a balcony where the family bedrooms were located. Everything was made of sun-dried brick, and plants hanging in strategic places around the courtyard made things homey and attractive. Caleb's aunt Helah was good at making their house pleasant and appealing, and Caleb always felt at home when he came into the sunny courtyard. Today was no different.

"I'm home!" Caleb called as he went to get a drink of water from the large clay water jar near the kitchen. "Anybody here?"

"I'm glad you've arrived," Aunt Helah smiled at her nephew. "Saarah needs help making the goat cheese. While you're doing that, you can listen to her recite her verses of Scripture and the Hebrew genealogies from Adam to David."

"Genealogies!" Caleb grumbled, not really thinking about what he was saying as he went to find his ten-year-old sister. "Always genealogies. What good are they, anyway?"

"They're good for developing your memory, and they help us to keep our heritage alive," a voice called from the pottery shop.

"Oh, you're home." Caleb half blushed as he realized his uncle Jabez had been listening. He stuck his head in at the wide doorway to the pottery workroom. "I didn't think you were here."

"Obviously not," came his uncle's reply.

The pottery shop was the family's livelihood. There was a never-ending need in Babylon for vessels made of clay. Water pots, jars for oil, and clay lamps were made in the shop and sold in the marketplace where Caleb's family did business, just a few hundred paces down the street.

"The meal is almost ready," Helah called to Caleb. "Hurry and help Saarah, so you can be done by the time the food is ready."

Caleb hung his head respectfully. "Yes, ma'am. I'll get right on it." He didn't like being bossed around, but he loved his aunt and uncle. They were his only family now, and all he had ever really known.

While they formed the goat curds into cakes of cheese, Caleb listened to Saarah recite her verses, but his mind wandered. The only thing he could think of was his conversation with Isi and Tamzi about the Medes and Persians, but he tried not to think about them. *Uncle Jabez told me that God will be with His people to protect them. I wonder if that is true. I'm not even sure the Jews are God's chosen people anymore. If we are, why are we still living in a pagan city such as Babylon? Why aren't we living in the land of Judah? I've heard the reasons why, but I'm not sure I really believe them.*

2

The afternoon sun stretched its last rays of light into the family court-yard, painting the shadows of palm trees on the home's stuccoed mud-brick walls. Purple swallows swooped here and there in the deep-blue sky, catching their last meal of bugs. A rooster crowed somewhere up the street, signaling the end of another day.

Caleb sat down on the large rug in the family courtyard as his twelve-year-old sister, Saarah, put a steaming pot of lentil stew at its center. Her dark eyes and auburn hair were a good match for her pretty face. And she was a good girl. She was a real help to Aunt Helah in so many ways.

As Caleb waited, he stared up at the cloudless sky, now turning a deep, burnished blue. It was dry this time of year. The rainy season had come to an end, so the family could eat their meal out in the open air.

Uncle Jabez and Grandpa Obed came into the courtyard from the pottery shop. They washed their hands and sat down on the circular rug, too, ready to eat the evening meal. Though Grandpa was nearly blind, his health was still good.

Everyone waited for Grandpa to say the usual blessing in thanks for the food. He looked to heaven, his gray head growing bald with age.

"Blessed are You, oh Lord our God, Master of the universe," he said, "who nourishes the whole world in goodness, with grace, kindness, and compassion. He gives bread to all flesh, for His mercy endures forever. Amen."

The flatbread and stew Aunt Helah had prepared tasted delicious, and Caleb went to work on it immediately. He was halfway through the meal before he remembered the news he had heard from Tamzi's brother up on the wall. "The guards are saying the Medo-Persian army is on the march again," he announced between bites of bread. "People are saying they might even come here."

"I don't doubt it," Uncle Jabez said as he dipped a piece of bread into his bowl of stew, "but I wouldn't worry any, if I were you. This city is too well fortified. It's not likely any army will ever conquer it." He sounded confident, but the look on his face didn't match his words. Caleb had to wonder whether his uncle was being honest.

"It's getting late, but we've got a little time left before bed," Uncle Jabez announced as he finished his meal. "Come Caleb; let's see if we can finish that order of pots we're making for the Elishama family wedding feast."

Caleb stood to his feet and brushed the crumbs from his tunic. The family pottery shop was just off the courtyard, and everyone worked to make it prosperous. Even Caleb's grandpa helped. He might have poor eyesight, but his hands were as strong as iron, and he could make a clay pot on the potter's wheel as quick as any other potter.

The three of them went right to work making up several large clay jars, which were to be used for grape juice at the coming wedding feast. Uncle Jabez and Grandpa Obed put large lumps of soft clay on their potter's wheels and then spun the wheels with their feet by turning the flat circular stones at the base of the wheels. Caleb lit several oil lamps, put some clay and a little water in the kneading trough, and then took his sandals off. By walking around barefoot in the clay, he mixed it, so it would be moist and smooth for his uncle and grandfather to use in making pots.

"Peace be to you," a voice called from the courtyard gate.

"Come in, Tamzi," Caleb shouted. "We're in the pottery shop."

"*Oooh*, that's nasty!" Tamzi made a face when he saw Caleb in the kneading trough with clay oozing up between his toes.

Caleb grinned. "It's not so bad. Why don't you join me? If we both work at it, I'll get done faster. Then maybe we can go down to the river and get some fish for breakfast."

"All right." Tamzi made a face again and took off his sandals. He stepped gingerly into the clay as though it might get him dirty, and both boys had to laugh at that. After several more minutes of working together, they took a knife and cut through the clay to see if there were any large lumps in it.

"Looks pretty good," Uncle Jabez glanced at the finished clay in the trough but kept his potter's wheel spinning. "Why don't you boys load the kiln with the jars we made today and then build a fire in it? After that, you can go."

"Thanks!" Caleb grinned in the lamplight and stepped into a large basin of water next to the kneading trough. "Here, clean your feet like this," he told Tamzi as he took a stick and scraped the red clay off his feet. It took a while to get the gooey clay off and then a bit longer to wash off the rest of the clay with water from the basin. When they were done, their feet were still stained with the clay, and Tamzi frowned.

"Don't worry," Caleb said. "The stain goes away in the morning if you wash your feet again. I have to do this almost every day."

The boys carefully carried the finished clay jars to the mud-brick kiln and lined them up along the circular walls inside of the oven. "Now, take this stick and light it with the coals from the kitchen oven," Caleb told Tamzi as he threw in some chucks of black pitch stacked by the kiln. He arranged some dry tinder in the center of the kiln and then took the firestick Tamzi handed him. "Man those bellows over there," he pointed to a wood-and-leather box at one side of the kiln. "When the flame gets brighter, step on that box very gently, so the fire can get some air. But be careful not to put the fire out."

Caleb and Tamzi worked together; before long, the blocks of pitch roared into flame, making the kiln hotter than hot. "We're leaving now!" Caleb called to his uncle as he and Tamzi scampered out the gate. Fishing lines in hand, they ran down the street to one of the many canals that crisscrossed the city of Babylon.

When they got to the canal, the moon was already above the city walls. The boys pulled some fishing strings out of their pockets and baited pieces of bone with some meat before throwing out their lines.

Caleb really liked to fish, especially at night when it was cool. The fish were easier to catch when it was dark, and he and Tamzi could talk while they were waiting for the fish to bite. The talk of war came up again and again and so did school, which would soon be starting up again for the boys. Tamzi would go to a government school, and Caleb would take classes from a scribe in the Jewish settlement.

Within an hour, the boys had caught several fish on their lines and then headed for home. Back in the family courtyard, they cleaned the fish and hung them up to dry by the kiln. The boys then sat down by the courtyard's clay oven to listen as Grandpa told stories about the lost kingdom of Judah.

"Those were terrible days," Grandpa Obed said sadly. His dim eyes stared past the flickering flames that danced up through the oven's iron grate. "Almost no one was doing what was right in the eyes of the Lord," he added with a sigh. "Oh, some tried, but they were treated badly. The rich would rob the poor of what little they had. If you didn't like someone, you just made up a story about some supposed crime the person had committed and then took him or her to court for it. If the rumor was bad enough, the person was stripped of everything he or she owned and sent to prison. Many were whipped horribly in the prisons, and some were even starved to death. No one was safe, especially the godly priests and the prophets of the Lord."

Grandpa Obed had told these stories many times before, but Caleb had never heard his voice quaver with emotion like tonight.

3

Grandpa was a great storyteller, and Caleb liked listening to his stories more than anything. Uncle Jabez listened with respect to Grandpa Obed's stories too. It was customary to let the oldest family member tell stories at the evening fire.

"I was just a boy, no more than nine or ten at the time," Grandpa Obed said, "but I remember the prophet Jeremiah would come to our house sometimes. He was such a good man and tried to encourage us, but we always felt so bad for him. I remember hearing my father talk with Jeremiah late into the night. They always thought I was sleeping, but I would creep up in the shadows as close as I could to hear what they were saying.

"I didn't understand everything they talked about, but it was clear to me that the king of Judah was a weak man. Jeremiah said he listened too much to the young advisers in his court, who were wicked men. Jeremiah told them the king of Babylon was going to come and attack Jerusalem, but they just laughed at him and told the king to throw him in prison."

Caleb noticed a tear steal down his grandpa's cheek. It made him sad to see Grandpa this way, knowing that once upon a time he had been just a boy too. Of course, everyone had been little at one time in their lives, but it was hard to imagine Grandpa as a young boy.

"Our people were blind to the message Jeremiah was trying to give us," Grandpa continued. "My father and mother knew he was right, but what were they among so many? Most folks believed the lies of the false prophets who were telling the king exactly the opposite of what Jeremiah was saying." Grandpa's eyes looked sad in the light of the fire.

"Unfortunately, everything happened just as Jeremiah said it would. King Nebuchadnezzar laid siege to our city. He broke down Jerusalem's walls and hauled us all away in chains to Babylon," Grandpa's voice quavered again. "Jerusalem was destroyed because our people forsook Jehovah."

The flame had died down in the oven now. The hour was late. Tamzi had already fallen asleep on the rug, and Caleb could hardly keep his eyes open. However, somewhere in his foggy mind where sleep begins, he could hear his uncle speaking.

"What you've said about our past is true," Uncle Jabez said, "but all is not lost. God is good. There is yet one prophecy to be fulfilled."

. . . . . .

Sabbath came and that meant Caleb's family got a break from the work in their pottery shop. It also meant they went to worship in the local synagogue as they did every week. Caleb liked being in the synagogue— a chapel-like place for worship that got its start in Babylon during the days of the great prophet Ezekiel. There were many other synagogues in Babylon, but Caleb's family always attended the one in the Jewish Quarter where they lived.

The women and girls sat on one side of the aisle, and the men and boys on the other. Saarah was sitting with Aunt Helah, and her friend Jemi was with her. Caleb thought Jemi was the nicest of Saarah's friends.

Everyone in the congregation greeted one another warmly and then sang the thirty-third psalm together:

"By the word of the LORD the heavens were made,
And all the host of them by the breath of His mouth. . . .
Let all the inhabitants of the world stand in awe of Him.

For He spoke, and it was done;
He commanded, and it stood fast. . . .
The counsel of the LORD stands forever,
The plans of His heart to all generations.
Blessed is the nation whose God is the LORD,
The people He has chosen as His own inheritance" (verses 6, 8, 9, 11).

Zaccai, a local Jewish scribe, then got up and read from the writings of the prophet Jeremiah. The message was a hopeful one and sounded very much like the things Grandpa Obed and Uncle Jabez had been saying the night before. However, there was one part that caught Caleb's attention especially:

"For thus says the LORD: After seventy-years are completed at Babylon, I will visit you and perform My good word toward you, and cause you to return to this place. For I know the thoughts that I think toward you, says the LORD, thoughts of peace and not of evil, to give you a future and a hope. Then you will call upon Me and go and pray to Me, and I will listen to you. And you will seek Me and find Me, when you search for Me with all your heart. I will be found by you, says the LORD, and I will bring you back from your captivity; I will gather you from all the nations and from all the places where I have driven you, says the LORD, and I will bring you to the place from which I cause you to be carried away captive" (Jeremiah 29:10–14).

A buzz ran through the assembled congregation as Zaccai finished the reading, and Caleb saw that not everyone was glad to hear the news. Some frowned, and Caleb could hear some mumbling that the prophecies were too old to be believed. Grandpa Obed was one of the grumblers.

Caleb stared in surprise at everyone's reaction and especially Grandpa's. *Why aren't they more excited? Why aren't they happy to hear that the time of our captivity in Babylon is nearing its end? We have been little more than prisoners of war in Babylon for almost seventy years. Don't these people want to go back to Judah? Isn't that what every Jew wants?*

On the way home, Caleb listened as his grandfather and uncle argued about what the scribe had said that day in the worship service. "The Lord is punishing us for our nation's disobedience!" Grandpa Obed said adamantly.

"That's right," Uncle Jabez replied. "We can't deny it, but God is also merciful."

"Judah must pay for its sins," Grandpa growled. "The people abandoned the worship of the one true God. They worshipped pagan deities, and they sacrificed innocent children on the altars to their gods!"

"That's true," Uncle Jabez said quietly, "but God has promised if we confess our sins, He'll forgive us and restore us to the land of our fathers."

"That lazy, good-for-nothing king of Babylon will never let us go, and you know it." Grandpa stared straight ahead as he walked but clung to Caleb's arm as the boy guided him.

"But what about the prophecies?" Uncle Jabez kept on. "The time is almost up."

"Prophecies, prophecies. Who knows if we can believe them." Grandpa shook his head impatiently. "You know what a conditional prophecy is, my son?"

"Of course."

"Then you ought to know that Jeremiah's prophecy is one of them."

"We don't know that," Uncle Jabez insisted. "Don't you have faith in Jeremiah's writings? Don't you trust Zaccai and the other elders at the synagogue—even a little?"

Grandpa scowled. "I've lived most of my days in Babylon. No one's going to deliver us, I tell you! This is where I'll die."

Uncle Jabez said no more. It was no use arguing with Grandpa. When he got an idea in his head, it was like pulling teeth to get him to change his mind. *Why is he being so stubborn?* Caleb wondered. *Why doesn't he want to believe in Jeremiah's prophecy? What is he afraid of?*

When they got home, the midday meal was ready. Aunt Helah and Saarah had gone ahead of the others to prepare the simple meal. To go along with the usual flatbread, they had chickpeas, cucumbers, and some dried fish. A piece of melon finished off the meal.

After the Sabbath meal, Tamzi came over, and the two boys went for a walk along one of the canals. The water level in the canals was fed by a system of locks and gates along the river that ran under the city wall and straight through Babylon.

During times of war, the gates to the canals were kept closed, but now they were open so that boats could transport goods back and forth on the waterways of the city.

The water in the canals was lower than usual as it was the dry time of year, but travel on them was just as busy as ever. Large boats made of reeds, which were shaped like round baskets, scooted back and forth across the canals. Small rafts made from wooden poles and more reeds also plied the waters, moving baskets of grain and bales of cotton. But it was the long canal boats that interested Caleb the most. With their sails stretched high on their masts and men rowing along each side, the boats could go anywhere on the waterways of Babylon's canal system.

The boys watched the boat traffic for a while and then walked to one of the gardens along the river. Suddenly, they saw some boys teasing an old beggar sitting near the canal. The man, obviously blind, had a clay cup sitting on the ground in front of himself. He knew the boys wanted the coins in his cup and was trying to stop them, but there seemed little he could do. He had a wooden staff and was swinging it back and forth above the cup.

"Go on. Get. Leave me alone!" he kept shouting, but this was just a game to the rowdy boys. First one boy would try to dart in and grab the cup and then another.

Caleb felt bad for the poor man. He knew it was just a matter of time before the boys got the cup with its coins. *It isn't right to treat people this way. I want to stop these hoodlums, but what can I do? There are six boys, and some of them are bigger than Tamzi and me.*

4

The day was a hot one, and sweat trickled down Caleb's back as his mind raced while trying to think what he should do. He and Tamzi were no match for the six boys surrounding the beggar, but he knew that shouldn't matter. Someone needed to stop those boys, and Caleb realized he and Tamzi were the only ones to do it.

"Hey! Leave the old man alone," he shouted at the ruffians.

The boys stopped and stared at Caleb, surprised that someone had caught them in the act. For a moment, they stood there as if not sure what to do next, but Caleb raised his fist and started running toward them. That was all the boys needed because they scattered in every direction, kicking the clay cup away as they went.

"Wow! That was scary," Tamzi exclaimed as the dust settled. "Why did you do that?" he added. "They could have whipped us, and you know it."

Caleb's knees were shaking. "Yeah, I guess. But we took them by surprise, and that gave us the edge."

Tamzi nodded, and his eyes grew big. "For now, maybe, but they'll be back."

Caleb knew Tamzi was right, yet he knew he had done the right thing.

He glanced nervously in the direction the boys had gone, but the boys had disappeared down the canal by now. "Come on," he said, "let's see how the old guy is doing."

When the blind man heard the boys approaching, he squinted in their direction, a look of fear on his face. "I don't want any trouble with you boys!" he said.

"We don't mean you any harm," Caleb assured him. "The other boys are gone. We chased them away."

The beggar sighed and leaned against the palm tree he was sitting under. His vacant stare followed their footsteps until they stood right in front of him. "Let us help you pick up your coins," Caleb said as he and Tamzi stooped to gather up the silver and copper pieces lying here and there in the dust.

"Thank you for your kindness, boys," the beggar said almost reverently. "May the God of Daniel bless you."

The boys continued on their way, but Caleb had plenty to think about. It made him feel good to have done something for the beggar; but he had been raised to do acts of kindness like this, so it was really no big deal. One thing the beggar had said puzzled him, though. He had asked God's blessings on them in the name of Daniel, and Caleb had to wonder who this Daniel was that he had been talking about.

Caleb had heard stories about a man named Daniel who had been a famous prophet in the palace during the days of King Nebuchadnezzar. But that had been a long time ago.

Nebuchadnezzar has been dead for twenty some years. Are these two Daniels one and the same?

And the bigger question: Is the prophet Daniel even alive any longer? I'm not sure it even matters, but it is interesting to think about anyway.

When Caleb got home that night, he asked his aunt about the prophet, but she could tell him little. "I'm sure he must be dead by now," she said. "It's been so long since anyone has seen him. I think I may have met him once when I was a little girl, but he was old even then. Honestly, I don't remember much about it.

"Why don't you ask your uncle?" she added as she put some bread dough and yeast in a clay bowl. "He's at a meeting with the elders in the synagogue, but he'll be home soon. He could probably tell you what you want to know, one way or the other."

Caleb waited for his uncle but got tired and finally went up to bed for the night. By the time Uncle Jabez got home, it was late, and Caleb was nearly asleep. "You still awake?" Uncle Jabez asked as he came into Caleb's room and sat down on the floor by his mat.

"Yes." Caleb rubbed his eyes and sat up. The moon was high in the sky. It sent a gentle stream of light through the small window in Caleb's room, making an eerie white square on the floor.

"Helah said you had some questions about an old Jewish prophet who used to live here in Babylon."

"Uh-huh," Caleb yawned. "Tamzi and I met an old beggar down by the river today. We chased some boys away who were trying to rob him, and he blessed us for it. It was a little bit strange the way he did it, though."

"What do you mean?"

"Well, he asked 'the God of Daniel' to bless us." Caleb pulled his knees up to his chest to stay warm. Nights could get surprisingly cool, even this time of year.

"So, I was just wondering if you know who the beggar was talking about. Aunt Helah said she may have seen Daniel when she was young."

"Yes, I know a bit about him." Uncle Jabez stroked his beard. "Like Helah, I saw him years ago, before he disappeared from public life. He was at our synagogue, telling some stories about his days in the court of King Nebuchadnezzar. He was a handsome man, even in his later years of serving the king.

"I remember the thing that impressed me the most about him was the way he always put God first in everything, even with the things he ate. He told us about the time he and his three Jewish friends refused to eat the king's food and wine because it wasn't kosher. What courage! And I guess he did well in school too. He and his friends graduated from the royal academy with top honors above all the other students. That really impressed the king because he gave Daniel and the other three guys great jobs in the royal court."

"Wow! Sounds like he was a pretty smart guy." Caleb yawned again.

"Definitely," Uncle Jabez nodded. "But I think he became the most famous when King Nebuchadnezzar had a mysterious dream one night. Unfortunately, Nebuchadnezzar couldn't remember the dream when he awoke the next morning and was very upset because he sensed the dream was somehow very important."

Caleb sat up a little straighter. "I bet you're going to say Daniel helped the king with the dream."

"He did." Uncle Jabez smiled at Caleb in the darkness. "Daniel prayed that God would show him the message in the king's dream, and that's exactly what happened. In a dream of his own, Daniel saw an image made of four different kinds of metal. It was exactly the same as King Nebuchadnezzar's dream. When Daniel told the king what he had seen and explained what it meant, the king was astonished. Not surprisingly, he made Daniel one of his highest-paid advisers, and the rest is history."

"Daniel must have been an amazing man!" Caleb said, staring off into the darkness.

"He was," Uncle Jabez nodded. "Unfortunately, most of us never knew him personally. Even during his best years, our people rarely saw him. He was a very busy man working in the palace. People like us don't get chances to spend much time with royal advisers, even if they're Jewish ones."

"I suppose not." Caleb shrugged. "But you saw him when you were about my age?"

"Uh-huh. A little older, I guess. It was a just after the king had been restored to his throne. They say he went crazy like an animal and was gone from the palace for several years."

"Really? I never heard about that." Caleb didn't feel sleepy at all with these kinds of stories.

"Well, that's probably because most Babylonians think it's bad luck to talk about stuff like that," Uncle Jabez said. "But you know the really surprising thing about that story? King Nebuchadnezzar finally decided he wanted to worship the one true God."

"Yeah?"

"Yes, and when he made that decision, God gave him back his sanity."

"Everybody must have been shocked at that," said Caleb. "Do you think Daniel had something to do with that?"

Uncle Jabez nodded. "I'm sure he did. He had much to do with most of the major decisions King Nebuchadnezzar made late in his life."

"I wish I could have met Daniel," Caleb said a bit wistfully. "He must have been quite a guy."

"That he was." Uncle Jabez yawned too. "You know, it's a shame. After King Nebuchadnezzar died, things kind of fell apart in the palace."

"It did? How?"

"There was lots of confusion about who should be the king at that time, and in the middle of it all, Daniel disappeared from public life. One king after another sat on the throne, some of them lasting only a few months. Not until Nebuchadnezzar's son-in-law Nabonidus came to power did things get a bit better, but now Nebuchadnezzar's grandson is in charge, and it's worse than ever. King Nabonidus is never in Babylon, so he leaves Belshazzar to run things, and that's what worries everyone."

5

Caleb glanced at his uncle. "What ever happened to Daniel?"

Uncle Jabez shook his head. "I don't know. It's been years now. I haven't heard any news that he died, but I can't imagine he's still alive either. If he is, he's very old. Much older than Grandpa Obed even."

"That's strange." Caleb squinted in the darkness. "If Daniel was that famous, you'd think people would have heard about him dying."

The conversation lulled as the night sounds pressed in around the uncle and nephew. Crickets still chirped. A lone screech owl shrieked its mournful call over the adjoining rooftops, and a dog barked somewhere down the street.

Uncle Jabez got to his feet. "It's late, Caleb. I'd better let you get some sleep. We've got to be up early in the morning if we want to make sure that order is filled for the Elishama family."

After he left, Caleb thought about everything Uncle Jabez had said. Certainly this prophet Daniel had been a real person, not just the stuff heroes and legends are made of. He was a famous man in Babylon, a big shot in the government, and a Jew. But the biggest question still wasn't answered in Caleb's mind: *Is Daniel alive somewhere among the hundreds of thousands in Babylon? Maybe, just maybe, he is.* With his whole heart, Caleb wished he could meet him. As he pondered this thought, he fell asleep.

The next morning Caleb was up bright and early to help his uncle and grandfather finish the orders for the wedding. There were small clay pots and large ones, but the most important ones were the huge jars that would be used for grape juice at the wedding. Stone jars were used in many places; but in Babylon, stone for making jars and pots was scarce, so clay was more common.

Caleb liked to work in the pottery shop, even if the hours were long. Classes at the synagogue had just ended for the next few weeks because the fall harvests were in full swing. That meant Caleb would have more time to help his family in the shop and more time with Tamzi.

Caleb had already hitched Boaz, the family donkey, up to a cart and was just loading the last of the clay jars when Tamzi came running into the family courtyard. "Caleb! Caleb!" he shouted. "There's news about the Medo-Persian army. They have beaten us at the Battle of Opis!" He bent over to catch his breath. "King Nabonidus has fled, and the army came back last night with their tails between their legs. They have lots of wounded soldiers with them."

"I don't get it!" Caleb looked stunned as he climbed down from the donkey cart. "How did they get beat? They looked well equipped when they left three months ago."

"No one really knows." Tamzi began to get his wind back, but he looked as frightened as if he had fought in the battle himself. "It's hard to tell how badly they were beaten, Caleb, but the army looks gloomy."

Caleb couldn't believe his ears. "Why don't you ask them?" He wanted to laugh and he would have, but Tamzi looked so serious.

"Well, that's just it," Tamzi exclaimed. "No one's talking. King Nabonidus ordered his officers not to say anything about the battle. But it doesn't really matter," he said dejectedly, as though this were the worst day of his life. "Judging by the numbers of soldiers who came home, they must have lost thousands and thousands of soldiers."

Caleb thought about all those Babylonian soldiers dying, and it made him feel sad. His own father had died while fighting in King Nabonidus's army at the Battle of Tema.

"What's going to happen now?" he stared at Tamzi anxiously. "Do you think Cyrus will come here next?"

" 'Fraid so." Tamzi nodded. "You can bet he's already setting his sights on Babylon. The guards on the wall say it's inevitable."

"But what about the Median Wall?"

"That won't stop Cyrus now that he's whipped Opis, because Opis is the only defense for the wall."

Caleb's face fell. "What about Sippar? It's a lot closer to us than Opis—only a few days' journey north of here."

"Sippar?" Tamzi shrugged. "It's nothing compared to Babylon. It won't put up much of a fight. Come on!" He grabbed Caleb's sleeve. "My brother is at the royal armory, working on the war engines. He'll tell you everything."

"OK, but I have to deliver these pots for my uncle. Why don't you help me, and then we'll bring the donkey cart back home before we go?"

The boys hurried off as fast as old Boaz would take them. He was a stubborn old donkey, so the going was slower than Caleb would have liked. Also, the cart was full of pots. The last thing Caleb wanted was to break any of them.

When the boys finally arrived at the armory next to the military commons, the place was humming like a beehive. Generals strategized with engineers to make the best use of the latest military weapons. Soldiers worked side by side with blacksmiths and carpenters to design the machines they would need to fight the army from the top of the walls of Babylon.

Massive stone catapults were being built with huge wooden beams and slings made from rope as thick as a man's wrist. Catapults for throwing stones and spear-throwers loaded with a battery of six giant spears were being tested on targets along a dirt embankment. Barrels of oil were being hauled to braziers above the gates where the oil would be heated and dumped on the enemies below. And, of course, tens of thousands of arrows, swords, and pikes were being made at the metal forges.

The morning passed, and the two boys helped do whatever they were asked. One of the blacksmiths gave them a bunch of arrows to sharpen on a grindstone. They helped pour oil into barrels and then led oxcarts loaded with the barrels up the steep ramps to the top of the city wall.

Tamzi stayed to work longer, but Caleb had to go home to help in the shop. While on the way, he passed through the marketplace and stopped to listen to several merchants talking about the Medes and Persians.

"I knew it would come to this," an old gray-bearded tanner fumed. "If our military was doing its job, we would have finished the Medes and Persians off a long time ago."

"That's right," a vegetable vendor retorted. "Gone are the days when Babylon was the terror of Mesopotamia. Nobody is afraid of us anymore."

"We deserve it, though," the tanner scowled. "Now everybody wants a piece of us. We've been sitting inside these walls for years and doing nothing, daring the world to come knocking on our door!"

"Yeah, well, King Belshazzar is nothing like his grandfather Nebuchadnezzar," the vegetable vendor said. He glanced around the marketplace and then lowered his voice. "The only thing His Highness wants to do now is party all the time."

"You both worry too much!" A fat butcher joined the conversation as he hung a goat carcass up on a meat hook in his stall. "No one's going to touch us inside these walls. How are they gonna get in?" he snickered.

Caleb didn't stay to hear more. Even the butcher's laugh didn't make him feel secure. Too much was happening too fast. The Medes and Persians were coming.

He hurried home, thinking about what he had seen and heard that morning. It was clear that some in Babylon were very much afraid of the approaching Medes and Persians. Then again, others, such as the sentries on the wall, were sure Babylon had nothing to worry about.

But try as he might, Caleb found himself growing more and more worried about an invasion. Babylon was not a godly city. No one in Babylon even knew about the God of heaven. The people were pagans, so they wouldn't know that Jehovah could help them. They would be praying to the gods of Babylon—especially Tammuz, Ishtar, and Marduk.

The thought of an invasion made Caleb feel scared and even desperate. *There is a good chance Babylon is going to fall, and if it does, the Jews will likely be destroyed too. It is enough to drive a guy crazy. But what can I do? I'm just one boy among thousands of people in a huge city.*

Then Caleb's thoughts turned to the God of his fathers. *Jehovah can help me and my family if He wants to. The question is, will He? After all, we are living in a foreign city full of idol worshipers.*

"Please help us, Lord," Caleb prayed, and he began to quote one of his favorite psalms:

"Happy is he who has the God of Jacob for his help,
Whose hope is in the LORD his God,
Who made heaven and earth,
The sea, and all that is in them" (Psalm 146:5, 6).

6

The metropolis of Babylon was a whirlwind of activity that week. Twice more Caleb and Tamzi found the time to go to the armory to help with the war preparations. Guard towers were stocked with weapons of every kind. The war engines were being rolled up the steep ramps to the walls high above, and huge platforms on the walls were loaded with ammunition.

There was no shortage of help for the approaching invasion; but the more Caleb saw, the more afraid he became. Everywhere he went people were arguing about what would happen next. Some felt sure that the Medes and Persians would conquer Babylon, but many were sure everyone would be secure behind the city's massive walls.

On Sabbath, Caleb was glad to go walking along the canals of Babylon again, and Tamzi went too. Adventures along the canal were the best way to get his mind off the thoughts of impending war. The city of Babylon was so big it had walls that were miles long. The canals themselves crisscrossed the city like patterns in a woven rug, with fields and marshes scattered here and there between.

"Let's see how that blind beggar is doing," Caleb told Tamzi as they neared the spot where they had chased away the bullies. "I wonder if the boys ever came back to bother him."

They found the old man, and he was having a hard time throwing out a line to catch a fish for his supper. It was a windy day, so the line kept blowing away in the wind and getting caught among the tall reeds along the bank of the canal.

Caleb retrieved the fishing line, put another piece of bait on the hook, and then went to a spot along the canal where he could wade out into the reeds. He threw out the line again; within a few minutes, he had a big fish up on the bank of the canal.

Tamzi scraped the scales off the fish with a knife from his belt, while Caleb got some dry reeds to build up the beggar's cooking fire. While the fish cooked on the coals, the boys talked with the blind man. He was obviously homeless; with hair was almost as white as snow, his deep-set eyes were now glazed a milky-white from blindness.

"Tell us a story," Caleb said, scooting closer to the beggar.

The old man smiled. "All right, what would you like to hear?"

Tamzi's eyes lit up. "Tell us about the days when you were young."

"Yeah," Caleb chimed in. "What's your name, and where did you grow up?"

"My name is Allamu, and I come from a poor family of peasants. I was raised in the east, near Bisitun, in the mountains of Elam. When I was still quite young, I was already different from my friends. I wanted to see the world, and to my mother's dismay, I left home to make my 'fortune,' as I called it. I was as poor as I could be, with absolutely no money, but I found a merchant who would let me travel with his caravan in exchange for help in watering and feeding his camels. When we traveled, I walked, of course, without a camel or donkey even to ride on. But I had travel fever in my blood, and that was enough for me."

Allamu turned to the fire and smacked his lips at the aroma of the fish baking on the coals. "Is that fish done yet?" His face lit up expectantly.

"Not yet." Caleb turned the fish over on the red-hot coals.

"*Mmm*, sure smells good," Allamu added and then returned to his story. "I had always wanted to come west to a city such as Babylon, and when we arrived one fine day in the metropolis, I stayed.

"I started working at the caravansary where our caravan stopped for a week, because that was what I knew how to do—take care of animals.

It was all I had ever known as a boy growing up. But that grew old fast. I figured I hadn't come this far just to water camels and clean up after them. So I tried my hand working for the cook at the caravansary. I didn't look or smell very good with the one tunic I owned, so I took the two pieces of silver I managed to save and bought a new tunic. You know, something suitable for one who was going to be serving rich merchants who stopped at the caravansary. I didn't know it then, but that turned out to be the best move of my life."

"Really? How's that?" Caleb took the broiled fish off the coals with a stick and handed it to Allamu on a palm leaf.

"Well, it happened like this"—Allamu smelled the fish as he held it gingerly in his hands and waited for it to cool—"one night I was serving these three merchants dressed in their fine robes, and one of them took notice of me. 'What's a handsome young man like you doing in a place like this?' he said.

"His compliment took me by surprise, I guess. I didn't know what to say. No one had ever said anything like that to me." Allamu stopped to pull pieces of the broiled fish off with his fingers and put them in his mouth.

"Go on. Go on!" Caleb and Tamzi said impatiently.

The beggar nodded. "I'm getting to it. Hold your horses, boys." He smiled as if reliving the moment from so long ago. "So anyway, the merchant asked me if I wanted to work for him at his estate."

"And you said yes?" Caleb was really engrossed in the story now, as if he were Allamu himself those many years ago.

Allamu took another bite of the fish. "That's right; and from then on, things got a lot better for me. I became one of the servants in the merchant's household and worked my way up until I became the steward of his kitchen."

Tamzi poked at the coals of the fire. "You must have been paid well for that job."

"Oh, I did all right, but it didn't end there. When my boss, Aariz, invited some government officials over for a fancy banquet, I was the one in charge, of course, to make sure everything was perfect for the meal.

"Anyway, one of King Nebuchadnezzar's advisers was there. His name was Zaidu, and he took a liking to me as well. To make a long story short, I eventually went to work for him and became his personal attendant."

"*Whoa!*" Caleb whistled. "All the way from peasant boy to being a personal attendant of the king's adviser."

Allamu smiled. "That's how I felt, and all before I turned twenty-five."

Caleb nodded at Tamzi. "We'd trade places with you any day, wouldn't we?"

"I know I would." Tamzi grinned. "It sure sounds exciting to me!"

"Well, it was. And for a few years, I did well there, but it didn't last." Allamu finished the fish and tossed the bones toward the fire.

"Really?" Caleb stirred the last of the dying embers. "Why not?"

"My master Zaidu was involved in a revolt against the king and was executed. His estate was confiscated by the royal family, and I lost my job."

Caleb whistled again. "Really? Wow! Where did you go then?"

"I went to work at the brick kilns on the Plains of Dura. It was a real change for me. So much had happened so fast, but I was just glad to have a job and happy to be away from the royal court."

"Really? Why?" Tamzi looked surprised.

Allamu picked at his teeth with a small stick. "I was afraid I might be blamed somehow or wrongfully connected with Zaidu's rebellion. I had known nothing of the attempted coup, but, of course, anyone can be a suspect in the government's court."

Caleb stared at Allamu. He felt bad for the old man. Working at a brick kiln, in the sweltering heat of the blast furnaces, was a backbreaking job and a real loss in status for a man who had been the steward of a royal adviser.

"You said the kilns were on the Plains of Dura." Caleb's eyes lit up with a sudden thought. "I was wondering, do you remember anything about the image King Nebuchadnezzar built on the Plains of Dura years ago? That really tall one they said was made of gold?"

Allamu smiled. "I remember it well. It was so tall it could be seen a day's journey away."

"A day's journey. Wow! It must have been gigantic."

"It was a monster, all right. Sixty cubits high, as I recall. It was built to honor Marduk, the chief god of the Babylonians, but I think it was more in honor of King Nebuchadnezzar. After the attempted revolt, I think he wanted everyone to know he was still king. It's why he gave the decree ordering every official in the empire to come to his ceremony in honor of the image. It's why he demanded that everyone bow to the golden image on the Plain of Dura. Satraps, governors, judges, magistrates—everyone who was anyone had to show up."

"All of them bowed?" Caleb asked. "I thought there were a few who didn't."

Allamu nodded slowly. "That's true. Actually, if I remember right, there were three."

7

The late afternoon shadows stretched long on the banks of the canal. The coals of the fire had nearly burned themselves out, yet Caleb knew the story wasn't finished.

Caleb put some more reeds on the coals and blew on them to fan the flames to life. "My family has told me that story many times," he said, settling back down by the fire. "They said it was three young Jews who wouldn't bow—Shadrach, Meshach, and Abed-Nego."

"You know that story?" Allamu smiled.

Caleb nodded, but Tamzi shook his head. "I never heard it before," he said. "Who were those guys?"

"They were three Jews who worked for the king in his palace court," Caleb added. "Experts on the laws and culture of the Babylonian government."

"They were the ones who didn't bow?" Tamzi got a funny look on his face.

"Yeah, they defied the king and refused to bow to his image."

"That's right," Allamu jumped in to continue the story. "King Nebuchadnezzar was hopping mad about it, too, and called the three men forward to the dais where he was sitting. 'Why have you disobeyed my command to bow to the golden image?' he demanded.

" 'We worship the God of heaven,' they said. 'He's the Creator of all things, and we can't worship anyone but Him.'

" 'But I'm your king, and I've ordered you to bow!' he shouted. The king was really, really mad by this time. 'If you don't bow, I'll burn you alive in a furnace.' " Allamu was reliving the moment as if it had happened only yesterday. "The brick kilns were already being heated up not far away, and black smoke was billowing from their stacks," he added.

"So the three guys bowed, right?" Tamzi asked excitedly.

"They did not." Allamu swatted at a mosquito buzzing close to his face. "They told the king they would rather burn than worship his gods."

"What?" Tamzi's jaw dropped. "Were they crazy? Who in their right minds would say such a thing? Didn't they believe the king would do what he said?"

"I don't know whether they believed him or not, but he kept his promise," Allamu replied. " 'Heat up the furnace seven times hotter than usual!' the king screamed. 'Roast those boys for their insolence!' "

Tamzi stared at Allamu in disbelief and then turned to Caleb. "Why would they do that?" he asked incredulously. "Why would they defy the king like that?"

Caleb shrugged. "Because they wanted to be faithful to Jehovah. Because they knew He could protect them, if He wanted to."

"Who could protect them?"

"Jehovah," Caleb said, looking straight at Tamzi. "The same God I serve."

"The God you serve? Your God could save them?"

"That's right." Caleb didn't miss a beat. "He's the God of all things and Sovereign of the universe. He has all power in heaven and earth to do whatever He wants, whenever He wants. He can help those who call on Him."

"But how did they know He would do it?"

"Because He's done it before. He's saved the people who serve Him many times before, and they knew it."

"But what if it was all a lie? What if your Jehovah decided not to save them?"

"That didn't matter to them. They had always worshiped Him as their

God, and they weren't about to dishonor Him now just because some raging king ordered them to do it."

Tamzi frowned. "So the king threw them in the furnace?"

"He did," Allamu interrupted after realizing Caleb had taken over his story. "King Nebuchadnezzar ordered his biggest, strongest guards to take those three guys, tie them up with rope, and throw them in a kiln furnace."

Tamzi could only shake his head. "You saw all that?"

"I did. Unfortunately, I was one of the workers ordered to throw in more fuel—bundles of straw soaked with oil. We had to climb up the stairs outside the kiln, so we could throw the bundles into the smokestack. It was superhot. I tried not to get too close to the chimney, or I would have been barbecued in an instant! I felt really bad for those guys. I admired them for their courage, but what could I do? If I didn't obey, the foreman at the kilns would have probably thrown me in the fire with the three guys."

"Wow! What a waste," was all Tamzi could say.

Allamu gave a half smile, and so did Caleb. "Yeah, well, the story doesn't end like you think. It has a happy ending."

Tamzi stared in amazement at Allamu and then at Caleb. "It does?"

"Yes!" Allamu looked almost triumphant, as though this was a story he was telling about one of his own gods. "When those boys got thrown in the furnace, they fell down on the sand at the bottom of the kiln. But then the smoke cleared a bit, and we saw them get up and start walking around."

" 'Walking around'? What are you talking about?" Tamzi got up on his knees. He was really confused now. "How did they walk around? They were burning up!"

"You'd think so," Allamu nodded, "but that's exactly what they did, and they were talking to each other like they weren't even in the furnace."

"Wait a minute. Wait a minute." Tamzi turned to Caleb, his eyes nearly popping with surprise. "You don't mean to tell me they didn't die?"

"That's exactly what he's saying." Caleb nodded. "It happened, Tamzi. Thousands of people saw it." Caleb couldn't help grinning at Tamzi's reaction to the story.

"What happened then?" Tamzi kept shaking his head.

"That's the most amazing part," Allamu replied. "The king stood up from his throne. 'I thought we threw three men in the fire,' he shouted. 'Why are there four men in there? They're walking around unhurt, and the fourth one looks like the Son of God.' "

Tamzi was frowning now. " 'The Son of God'?" he asked. "Who's the Son of God?"

"It's Jehovah," Caleb said quietly.

"Jehovah? You mean your God? He was in the fire with the three guys?"

Caleb nodded. "That was Him. They knew their God could protect them, but they probably didn't think He would show up to be with them in the fire."

"Wow!" Tamzi stared at Allamu in disbelief. "And you were there to see it?"

"I was."

For a moment, no one said anything. The sun had set, turning the sky overhead a deep blue. Bats had come out for the evening, flitting here and there in their search for insects. Now and then a fish jumped out of the water flowing in the canal.

Caleb picked up a stick and poked at the fire to keep it going. "Allamu, the day we scared those bullies off you blessed us in the name of Daniel's God," he said. "I've been wondering. Did you ever know someone important named Daniel?"

Allamu turned toward Caleb again in the gathering darkness. "I did." He paused and then went on, "I once knew a Daniel who saved the life of my master Zaidu. The king's courtiers and advisers couldn't solve a mysterious dream King Nebuchadnezzar had—one he had quite forgotten. And that was the problem." Allamu raised his eyebrows. "Zaidu was one of the advisers. But when he and his cronies failed to come up with an explanation for a dream nobody knew anything about, the king was madder than mad. 'Kill them all!' he growled. 'I've no use for phonies in my court.' "

"And did he?" Tamzi was back in the conversation again.

"He killed a few, and that's where Daniel comes into the picture." A faint smile flitted across Allamu's face. "You see, Daniel was also an adviser to the king and was scheduled to be executed too. However, he asked for time to solve the mystery and then came back the next day with a bizarre story. He claimed his God had showed him the king's dream, and apparently, He had. At least, it appeared so, because he knew every detail of the king's dream. The king was so impressed he set the advisers free. Then he promoted Daniel to a high position in his court; he became his right-hand man and his best friend, I might add."

"Really?" Tamzi was captivated by Allamu's story.

Unfortunately, the hour was late, and the boys had to go home. Caleb couldn't remember having had a better time. A lot of questions had been answered for him; for now, that was enough.

8

That night Caleb told Uncle Jabez and Aunt Helah about his day with Allamu. "He's a pretty neat character. He seems very smart, and not what I would expect in a blind beggar," Caleb told them. "You'd love his stories too. He knew Shadrach, Meshach, and Abed-Nego when he was younger. And he knew Daniel. Can I bring him home sometime for a meal?"

Aunt Helah smiled. "That would be a kind thing to do," and with that, Caleb went to bed.

The harvest had come and gone, so it was time for Caleb to go back to school again. It made no sense to him with the Medes and Persians on the warpath, but Uncle Jabez said he had to go. "We don't know what will come of the Medo-Persian invasion," he said, "but we do know you need an education, so it's off to school for now."

Caleb had been attending Jewish classes for boys and was learning how to read and write Hebrew. He already knew Aramaic, the language of Babylon and the Chaldeans who were the highly educated ones in the government courts. Caleb knew he had to know about mathematics and science, like the Babylonian schools taught, but mostly he wanted to hear about the history and religion of his people.

Before going to school, he had to eat his morning meal, say his prayers, and milk the family goats to have them ready for the goatherd, who would take them out to pasture. Then, of course, he had to help take the finished clay pots and jars to the marketplace. All this had to be done by dawn, so that by daylight he could be in his place with the other Jewish boys at the synagogue school.

The teachers in his school were strict. If he wasn't on time and didn't have his lessons memorized, they would give him more to do. But somehow none of that bothered him because the stories his teachers told were worth it all.

As a younger boy, he had learned all the genealogies of his people from Adam to the present. Now he was learning the lessons from the lives of the patriarchs and the prophets, the kings and the generals, and the priests and the judges. He was excited to hear about the sons of God who had been giants in the days of Noah. He was amazed that Abraham would pray for the people of Sodom who had stolen Lot's heart away.

His teachers impressed him with the faith of Jacob and Joseph and Moses. They told him about the ten plagues in Egypt, the crossing of the Red Sea by two million slaves, and the walls of Jericho that came tumbling down. They impressed him with the brave deeds of Gideon and Samson, and David's loyalty to a crazy king who wanted to see him dead.

But the failures of his people made his heart ache: they strayed from Jehovah to worship idols of wood and stone; they offered sacrifices to these pagan gods, sometimes even babies and children; and they persecuted the prophets and killed them because they didn't want to hear the prophets' messages of coming doom.

Elijah, Isaiah, and Jeremiah had braved the wave of wickedness sweeping across Israel and Judah, but it had seemed to be for nothing. Jerusalem had fallen just like the prophets said it would. Of course, those were the hardest stories to hear because this was why Caleb's people came to live in Babylon. They were still paying for the mistakes of their grandfathers and grandmothers, who had cared nothing for the God of heaven.

Tamzi wasn't a Jew, so he couldn't attend Caleb's school. He attended a Babylonian school; but after hearing Caleb talk about his classes, he admitted his own teachers were just plain boring. "The only things they talk about are the brutal battles between their hideous gods in the sky. They praise the armies of Babylon, who have butchered the nations of the earth. Worst of all, they make us sing dull songs about long lists of ancient kings from thousands of years ago."

"I wish I could go to school with you at the synagogue," Tamzi admitted one afternoon when he saw Caleb in the marketplace. "I think the stories of your people are much more interesting." He glanced around to make sure no one was listening and whispered, "The amazing things your God, Jehovah, has done make the gods of Babylon look like jokes."

Caleb thought about what Tamzi had said while he did his chores. He thought about it when he was in the marketplace selling clay pots and when he was in class each morning. He knew Tamzi was right. The ways of Jehovah were far beyond anything the people of Babylon could understand. The laws of God, if obeyed, could make God's people happy and holy. The stories from the Scriptures proved it was true.

News of the Medes and Persians being on the move kept dribbling into Babylon. It seemed like a horrible nightmare, but Caleb tried not to think about it. He continued to help his uncle and grandpa in the family pottery shop in the afternoon. Life had to go on. Every Jewish boy needed a skill he could use to make a living, and making clay pots was a good way to do it. But, of course, that didn't help Caleb much with the city of Babylon at risk. His mind was far away most days, and often he found himself wishing he could be up on the wall with Tamzi to watch for the Medo-Persian army.

The next Sabbath after the worship service, Caleb and Tamzi ran to the canal and brought Allamu home as they had promised. After a meal of fish, flatbread, and lentil stew seasoned with leeks, the blind beggar entertained them with more stories of his early days.

"Not long after the ceremony with King Nebuchadnezzar's golden image on the Plain of Dura, I got a new job working on a construction crew. I became a bricklayer and worked on the king's building projects all over Babylon. It was quite a change from the hot furnaces at the brick kilns and a far cry from directing servants on the estate of a government adviser. But I didn't care much. I was young and grew strong from the hard work. We got to work all over the city on projects that used different colored bricks. The city walls were made of yellow bricks, and the arching gateways were made of blue bricks. Red bricks were used for palaces, and white ones for temples. But it was the brightly decorated pictures of bulls, dragons, and lions that really turned heads, and I was given a chance to help design them."

Allamu smiled as if remembering every detail. "We built the bas-reliefs of Babylonian creatures right into the walls, and that became the most fun part of our job. Brown bulls, yellow dragons, and golden lions."

Caleb was seeing a new side of Allamu he hadn't seen before, but one thing bothered him. He was sad that a man with so many great stories could no longer see. "How did it happen, Allamu?" He was afraid to ask such a question, but he had to know. "How did you go blind?"

Allamu's smile slowly faded away. "I don't really know," he said sadly. "It was during those days as a builder that I knew something was wrong. Maybe I got some dust in my eye. Maybe I got a scratch on my eye or something. I don't know. My right eye went first, slowly growing dim like the darkness of dusk. When I finally went completely blind in that eye, the other one began to go too. I was terrified. It was unexplainable! Nothing like that had ever happened to me before. I went to doctors, but they couldn't do anything for me with their potions and poultices. They even tried magic; but nothing worked, and I went blind in the other eye too."

"I'm sorry," was all Caleb could say. Aunt Helah had tears in her eyes, and Uncle Jabez blew his nose. Even Tamzi felt bad.

"It's OK," Allamu sniffed. "The only bad thing anymore is that I have to beg for a living. That's the hard part."

The sun was low in the sky now, and Allamu asked the boys to take him back to the canal. The boys protested, but Allamu insisted. "It's my home, boys. It's all I know."

Aunt Helah put some flatbread and pomegranates in a basket for Allamu, and the boys took him back to his mat by the canal as he wished. The day had been a fun one for the boys as they listened to Allamu's stories, and it was hard to see him go.

But one thing was sure. Troubling days were ahead with the coming of the Medes and Persians, and Allamu's stories could hardly make a dent in that thought.

9

Dawn had just crossed over the eastern horizon as Tamzi came racing through the gateway of Caleb's family courtyard the next morning. Caleb had already milked the goats and was getting ready to take the new day's supply of pottery to the market.

"Let me help," Tamzi said as he loaded the clay pots and jars on the donkey cart. "I've got good news. I don't have school today, so I get to help my father in the warehouse of the royal archives. Do you want to come too? I know you have to go to class this morning, but my father says you can help this afternoon, if your uncle agrees."

Uncle Jabez said yes, and Caleb could hardly wait. He had never been to the archive warehouse. He had no idea what he and Tamzi would be doing, but whatever it was, he knew it would be fun. It had to be! From what Tamzi had told him, the warehouse was like a government museum.

The morning classes crawled by like snails, and it seemed like sheer torture to Caleb. Nothing could keep his attention. Not even the psalms they sang before class started or the stories about the prophet Elisha's miracles in the days of Israel's apostasy.

But the morning finally ended, and Caleb raced home to grab some flatbread and figs before running off to the warehouse. When he arrived, he found Tamzi with his father, taking inventory of war trophies.

The boys had a great time! Wooden crates full of exquisite vases and pottery had to be opened and recorded. Some were from Egypt. Others were from such cities as Nineveh and Sidon and Carchemish.

Other crates contained gold and silver idols from nations the Babylonians had conquered to the south. There was furniture made of ebony and ivory from the kingdom of Cush and jewelry of all kinds from Arabia.

After recording the relics on clay cuneiform tablets, some of them were repacked in crates, while others were stored on shelves in the warehouse. Later they would be used as decorations in the halls and rooms of the palace grounds.

For a while, the boys worked with Tamzi's father, Malik, but near the end of the day, he sent them to work by themselves unpacking crates in another chamber of the warehouse. Tamzi began by taking the lids off some heavy wooden crates in one corner. He whistled as he lifted out exquisite statues made of marble and then went to work recording them on his clay ledger.

Caleb climbed up on a stack of crates to examine some wooden cartons near the ceiling. Some were smaller, but some were very large. On the back side of one large wooden crate, he could see familiar characters printed in Aramaic. Then he saw yet another crate. As his gaze swept the area, he could see many, many crates. All were labeled the same: "War trophies from Judah," "Relics from Zedekiah's temple," and "Temple treasures from Jerusalem."

At first, he was confused as he mumbled through the pronunciation of the Aramaic phrases. But then his heart almost stopped, and his eyes got big when he realized the possible meaning of what he was seeing.

"Hey, Tamzi! Come up here," he called. "You've got to see this!"

Tamzi set down his clay tablet and wooden stylus and climbed up on the stack of crates to join Caleb.

"Do you know what these are?" Caleb gasped, with a look of sheer amazement on his face.

Tamzi shrugged as he read several of the Aramaic descriptions. "Looks like crates full of old artifacts. Isn't that what the words say?"

"That's right, except for one thing." Caleb continued staring at the crates. "I think they might be artifacts from my homeland."

Tamzi stared at Caleb blankly. "They're what?"

"I know it sounds crazy." Caleb scratched his head. "Do you think it's possible? Can the things in these crates be from my homeland of Judah. The writing on the crates sounds like it."

"Judah? Oh yeah, that's your homeland, isn't it?" Tamzi squinted at Caleb. "OK, so maybe they are. But how did the things in these crates get here?" It was obvious Tamzi had no clue what Caleb was talking about, and that didn't help any.

Caleb scanned the stack of crates along the wall again. "How did they get here? That's my point, Tamzi!" He was really getting excited. "I think these things might be national treasures taken from the capital city of Judah."

"You think so? When?" Tamzi was getting interested too.

"Maybe when King Nebuchadnezzar conquered Judah. It was years and years ago, certainly, but not in the days of ancient history. In my grandfather's lifetime, at least."

Tamzi raised his eyebrows at Caleb. "Really? Wow!"

"Yup!" Caleb ran his hand over the writing on one of the crates. "If it's true, we just made the discovery of a lifetime. Come on, let's ask your father about this," and off they went in search of him.

Maybe Malik can shed a little light on what is in the crates, Caleb thought. *Do the words on the outside of the crates show what is really inside of them? If the artifacts are the real deal, are they the same ones that were stolen from Jerusalem so many decades before? Why would they still be here in the archive warehouse?*

Caleb knew he was probably getting his hopes up for nothing. The crates were likely empty or filled with other artifacts by now. The sacred treasures from Jerusalem were, no doubt, long gone.

The boys found Malik and took him to see the crates. "*Hmm*, I've been working in the royal archives for more than fifteen years now, but I've never climbed up there to see what's in those crates." He shrugged. "I couldn't say how long they have been buried there among the other boxes. We don't come in here often."

He glanced at the late afternoon sunlight streaming through the small windows high in the warehouse wall. "We'll have to open them up another day, boys. It's late and time to go home."

"I'm going to ask Uncle Jabez about this," Caleb told Tamzi as he headed for home. "I just know those crates are full of treasures from the days of King Nebuchadnezzar's invasion. They've got to be!"

The more Caleb thought about it, the more wound up he got. Unfortunately, he had no real idea what kinds of treasures they might find in the crates. *Could there be some artifacts, made of gold and silver, from Solomon's temple?*

The bigger question may be, what kinds of things had been in the temple back in Jerusalem? For an answer to that, I will have to ask my uncle or one of the scribes in the synagogue. Then again, maybe I can read the Scriptures myself. I might find some clues there.

But again, in his heart, Caleb knew he was probably getting his hopes up for nothing. When they finally opened the crates in the warehouse, they would probably find only dust and scorpions instead of the priceless treasures he wished were there.

For now, he had to wait on Tamzi's father to open the crates; who knew when that would be? Malik and Tamzi were Babylonians, so they had no clear picture of the importance of this discovery. How could they, when they worshiped pagan idols such as Marduk, Tammuz, and Ishtar? They had never bowed before the God of heaven and earth, so how could they really appreciate the sacred things that had been in the Lord's temple at Jerusalem?

But Caleb had to be honest with himself too. He had heard stories about the destruction of Jerusalem many, many times, though he was not alive during those days. He had never seen the glorious temple in Jerusalem. He had never seen the gold and silver things in the sanctuary. Jerusalem had been destroyed long ago, and nothing could change that.

Even in his worship of Jehovah, he knew he didn't really understand God. The question was whether he would have a better understanding of who God was once they found the holy relics of the kingdom of Judah. Time would tell.

10

At the evening meal that night, the news of the day tumbled out—with Caleb doing most of the talking. Children were supposed to be quiet at meals, but Caleb was so excited he could hardly eat his lentil stew. He kept tearing off pieces of flatbread and pushing them into his mouth as he talked, and Aunt Helah finally had to remind him to keep his mouth closed while he was eating.

Uncle Jabez was very interested in the surprising discovery. "Is it possible?" he said as he stroked his dark beard. "Do the long-lost relics of Judah still exist? We know that conquerors often take the gods of the nations they defeat and put them in the temples dedicated to their own pagan gods. Remember the story about the ark of God's covenant being stolen by the Philistines, which was then put in the temple of Dagon? The Philistines believed that capturing the gods of other nations would give them power over their enemies." Uncle Jabez took a piece of flatbread, tore off a portion, and dipped it in the bowl of hummus at the center of the rug where they were sitting.

"The Babylonians are like that too," he added. "They think that capturing the gods of their enemies means the gods of Babylon are superior."

"But the relics of ancient Judah weren't gods," Caleb said. "They were sacred because they were used in the temple worship services of Jerusalem. We didn't worship them." He looked confused.

"Good point," Uncle Jabez replied, "but the Babylonians don't know that. They collected all of the sacred dishes and furniture, along with the idols of gold and silver that were being worshiped by Zedekiah, Jehoiachin, and Jehoiakim in Jerusalem. It's a sad thing, too, because King Josiah had gotten rid of all those pagan gods from such places as Ammon, Moab, and Sidon."

"That's right." Grandpa Obed finished his lentil stew and wiped his mouth on his sleeve. "King Josiah got rid of Molech and Chemosh and Ashtoreth, but all that ended when King Jehoiakim came to the throne."

"Why?" Caleb stared at his grandfather. "What happened?"

Grandpa shook his head. "He brought back all those foreign idols."

"How did he do that?" Caleb loved history, even though some parts of it were rather sad. "I thought he only reigned for a few years before Nebuchadnezzar invaded the land. How did he get everyone back into the worship of such hideous idols in such a short time?"

"Well, when people have worshiped pagan gods for so many years, and that's what they still want to do, even a good king such as Josiah couldn't help much."

"Really?" Caleb scooted closer to his grandfather, "Tell me about that," he added as Aunt Helah lit several oil lamps in the courtyard, and Uncle Jabez lay down on the circular rug to listen.

Grandpa Obed leaned against the wall, which he was sitting near. "Almost three hundred years after the kingdoms of Judah and Israel divided, King Josiah came to the throne," Grandpa said. "He was a good boy. That was clear even before he was crowned as king at the young age of eight. He had a good mother, but his father, Amon, was a scoundrel like his grandfather, King Manasseh, before him. Both rulers tested the Lord beyond the limits of mercy and compassion.

"King Manasseh didn't continue the good things his father, Hezekiah, had brought to the country. Manasseh communicated with the spirit world through magic and witchcraft. He worshiped every pagan idol from Tyre to Egypt and set up altars to these gods right in the sanctuary of the Lord's temple in Jerusalem. Even worse, he sacrificed his own children and burned them on these altars."

Grandpa Obed's voice quavered with great sadness. "I'm surprised the God of our fathers didn't send us into captivity during the days of wicked King Manasseh. Actually, he did allow Manasseh to be taken away in chains by the Assyrians. Fortunately, the king repented during his later years and was restored to his throne in Jerusalem, but it wasn't enough. His influence had driven the culture of Judah too far into sin, and most of our people never made it back to the worship of the one true God.

"King Manasseh's own son Amon was just as evil as his father, and the people killed him for it. Two years into his reign, some of his top men assassinated him right in the palace. I guess they had had enough of Amon's evil deeds. Then, wouldn't you know it? The people of Judah took those assassins and executed them too. The place was a mess!" Grandpa looked disgusted, but he wasn't finished.

"That's when Josiah was put on the throne. He was only eight years old at the time; but his heart was right, and the good priests and princes helped him. While he was still young, he ordered the destruction of every pagan idol and altar in the country. He cut down all the carved wooden poles dedicated to the gods. He destroyed all the high places where people worshiped their idols. He destroyed all the parks on the hills where wild parties were held, where people got drunk in the name of their gods, and where child sacrifices were made to Molech and Chemosh.

"King Josiah also asked Hilkiah the priest to clean and repair the temple. While laboring there, the workers found a copy of God's Law as recorded by Moses. In one of the scrolls, they read about the curses that would come to God's people if they abandoned the worship of Jehovah.

"The king was horrified at the messages of doom he discovered in the scrolls! In desperation, he ordered that the worship of God be restored in Jerusalem.

"In the end, a great reformation spread throughout the land, but it wasn't enough. The sins of the people were so great, and most did not fully return to the worship of the Lord. Secretly, they still worshiped their gods. They didn't honor the Sabbath. They were corrupt and cheated everyone they could—especially the poor. In their courts of law, judges took bribes to send innocent people to prison and even to death."

Grandpa Obed shook his head sadly. "We had a few short years of peace, but then Josiah died in battle, and from there everything went downhill fast."

Caleb didn't know much about this part of Judah's history. "Who came to the throne then?" he asked.

"Jehoiakim, one of King Josiah's sons," Grandpa Obed said. "Well, actually his younger brother Jehoahaz was the crown prince before Jehoiakim, but no one really remembers him as king because he lasted only three months. Judah had made a treaty with Egypt, but Jehoahaz was kind of ornery. He rebelled and broke the treaty as soon as he was put on the throne. That sealed his fate and, the pharaoh, Necho, promptly put him in prison."

"And that's when Jehoiakim came to the throne?"

"That's right. His name was actually Eliakim, but Pharaoh Necho changed it to Jehoiakim when he invaded Judah. I think he liked the sound of the new name better. It means 'Jehovah raises him up.'" Grandpa half smiled. "But I think Necho felt he had been the one to raise him up. The two of them had been friends for years."

"I wouldn't want to be either of those two kings," Caleb admitted.

"Those were hard times," Grandpa Obed admitted. "Unfortunately, Jehoiakim didn't get along any better with Babylon than Jehoahaz had with Egypt. The prophet Jeremiah told him to submit to the Babylonian king. He begged him to pay the taxes he owed, or the fierce Babylonians would come and destroy Jerusalem. Everyone would be taken captive as slaves to Babylon, he warned, but King Jehoiakim refused to listen."

"And it happened just like Jeremiah said it would," Caleb chimed in excitedly.

"That's right." Grandpa Obed heaved a tired sigh. "No one listened, especially King Jehoiakim. When Nebuchadnezzar finally showed up three years later, it was like a horrible nightmare. He took Jehoiakim captive and raided the royal treasury."

Caleb whistled. "I'm glad I wasn't living in those days!"

"Well, I was," Grandpa Obed grunted. "I was born just before the first invasion. During the next twenty or so years, the powerful Nebuchadnezzar returned to Jerusalem two more times. Neither King Jehoiachin nor King Zedekiah behaved themselves. Like King Jehoiakim, they both refused to pay their taxes to Nebuchadnezzar, and that was the final straw. On his second and third times through Jerusalem, King Nebuchadnezzar ransacked the city and holy temple and then finally burned the place to the ground."

"And brought the treasures to Babylon in the crates we found," Caleb said with a strange light in his eyes.

"Could be." Uncle Jabez sat up and yawned. He had been so quiet that Caleb almost forgot he was there. "Those crates at the warehouse may very well contain relics from ancient Judah," he said matter-of-factly. "Or they may contain nothing at all."

Caleb didn't want to think about that possibility. The idea that the artifacts in the crates could indeed be the long lost treasures of Judah was too exciting to ignore.

11

Uncle Jabez went to bed, but Grandpa Obed and Caleb stayed a while longer to talk. There was one lone lamp still burning in the courtyard, and the shadows from its flickering flame danced this way and that on the walls. Caleb watched absentmindedly as several moths fluttered dangerously near its flame.

"If the writing on those crates is real and is an accurate record of what's in them, you may have stumbled on an incredible find," Grandpa said with a twinkle in his eye.

"You think so?" Caleb felt himself beginning to shake from the cool night air. *Or am I just jittery about the biggest find of my life? The biggest find of the century! The idea that the precious treasures may still be hidden away in the warehouse of the royal archives is beyond my wildest imagination.* He was finding it very hard to remain calm.

Grandfather nodded. "Truth is, those relics may be all that's left of Jerusalem. Solomon's glorious temple is no more. The fine palaces he built are gone. The walls of the city are broken down, and the gates are burned with fire. And the long-lost treasures? By now, I'd say most Jews have forgotten that such treasures ever existed or were brought to Babylon at all. Those who have thought about it probably assumed the idols of gold, silver, and bronze were put in the Babylonian temples dedicated to Marduk and Ishtar. One would think the rest of the valuable stuff from Solomon's temple has long since been melted down. The precious metals they contained could always be used in the construction of temples and idols to the Babylonian gods."

Grandfather stood stiffly to his feet. "We'd better get some sleep, Caleb. You have school in the morning," and with that he shuffled off to bed.

Caleb went off to bed, too, but he couldn't sleep, not even when he lay down on his sleeping mat. Thoughts of glory were swirling in his head. The idea that some of the treasures from Jerusalem could remain untouched in a warehouse all these years was unthinkable!

Preposterous! Or is it reality? Grandfather said what I've believed all along and wanted to hear. What remains of Judah's culture may very well be in that storeroom.

But Caleb knew he was getting ahead of himself again. *No one actually knows what is in those crates. Except for the writing on the crates, of course. Then again the crates could have been unpacked years ago and may be empty now or even refilled with other artifacts.*

Caleb's mind darted back and forth, buzzing with a myriad of possibilities. *It was driving him crazy thinking about it! What if Tamzi's father reports the crates to the court officials? What if they open the crates and find the temple treasures inside after all? If that happens, the holy things may very well be taken away and disappear again—this time for good. In that case, they may never be seen by me and my people again.* The thought of such a thing almost made Caleb wish they had never found the crates.

Sometime before midnight Caleb finally dozed off. He dreamed of the ancient kingdom of Judah, the magnificent temple of Solomon with its white-robed priests, and many golden treasures hidden away in its secret chambers.

Caleb went back to school the next day, but he couldn't forget about the crates in the warehouse. Was it only yesterday that he and Tamzi had discovered them? It now seemed like ages ago.

He thought about the discovery the entire morning and wondered who he could ask about the lost treasures of Solomon's temple. Other than Grandpa he didn't know anyone at the synagogue who was old enough to have actually lived in the land of Judah. The destruction of Jerusalem had been several generations ago. He was sure there must be a few people in Babylon who were old enough to remember. The trouble was he didn't know how to find them.

When he arrived home for the noonday meal, Uncle Jabez was at the market, so he asked Aunt Helah if she knew anyone he could talk to about it.

"Well, I'm sure there are a few still living from the days of King Zedekiah who might know something about the lost treasures," she said. "If you can get them to talk. I don't know very many who have good feelings about those days. Most of them are bitter with the memory of it all. Many blame God for the destruction of Solomon's temple and Jerusalem."

Caleb was shocked at such an idea. "It wasn't God's fault the enemy came up to Judah and surrounded Jerusalem." he said. "It wasn't His fault that Nebuchadnezzar finally destroyed the city and everything in it." Caleb could feel himself getting angry. "It was the fault of our ancestors, our great-grandfathers and great-great-grandfathers! The kings of Judah wouldn't listen to Jeremiah! They rejected his prophecies and messages of warning, and the people just followed their example."

Aunt Helah stirred some salt and cumin seeds into a chickpea stew. "Where did you hear that?"

"From Grandpa."

"Well, Grandpa would remember a lot. He was a young man at the time. Of course, it was a long time ago. The years have a way of making us remember only what we want to remember."

Caleb stared at Aunt Helah. "What do you mean by that?"

"Just don't get your hopes up, Caleb. It's been a long, long time since that stuff was brought here from Jerusalem. Now go listen to your sister recite her memory lines from Scripture."

Caleb sat down on an overturned basket as he listened to Saarah repeat her lines.

Saarah repeated,

"Trust in the LORD, and do good;
Dwell in the land, and feed on His faithfulness.
Delight yourself also in the LORD,

And He shall give you the desires of your heart" (Psalm 37:3, 4).

Caleb knew these verses by heart. He tried hard to focus on his sister's voice to see if she was missing any words, but his mind wandered. He didn't want to admit that what Aunt Helah had said might be true, but she had a point. Nebuchadnezzar's invasion of Judah had happened a long time ago. The Jews had new lives in Babylon now. Only a few were old enough to remember Jerusalem, and digging up stories from the past may only make them feel bad. Jerusalem was gone, and nothing could change that.

His sister's voice droned on.

"Commit your way to the LORD,
Trust also in Him,
And He shall bring it to pass.
He shall bring forth your righteousness as the light,
And your justice as the noonday" (verses 5, 6).

Caleb wanted to believe the words his sister was reciting, but he had to wonder about Aunt Helah. *Does she have less confidence in the fulfillment of Jeremiah's prophecies than I do? I don't want to think so, but maybe her faith in God isn't as strong as it should be.* The possibility was there, and he had to admit it might be true.

Saarah recited the final lines.

"But the salvation of the righteous is from the LORD;
He is their strength in the time of trouble.
And the LORD shall help them and deliver them;
He shall deliver them from the wicked,
And save them,
Because they trust in Him" (verses 39, 40).

There was no doubt in Caleb's mind that God could do for His people what the psalmist said. The question was, would He do it?

"Come, children," Aunt Helah called. "Uncle Jabez is home. It's time to eat."

Caleb went to his usual spot on the circular rug in the corner of the courtyard. *I want to see the hidden treasures in the warehouse, but they may not be the most important things right now. Maybe the approaching Medes and Persians are. Nothing will make them go away—not the armies of Babylon, not the well-fortified walls of the city, and maybe not even God.*

The thought of such a thing made Caleb shiver, even in the hot afternoon sun. Things were about to get crazy in Babylon! He could feel it in his bones, but he tried not to think about it. He picked up some flatbread and tore off a piece. *Maybe a little food in my stomach will help.*

12

Day by day the tensions in Babylon were growing. As Caleb climbed the staircases to the top of the city wall and looked out across the metropolis of Babylon, everything looked peaceful enough. However, when he walked the busy streets below, it was quite another thing altogether.

Everyone was talking about the coming Medo-Persian army. Women argued about it when they drew water from the city wells. Men shouted back and forth in the marketplace and public amphitheaters. Children fought it out in the war games they played on the streets.

Discussions began to take on a different tone due to the strain of it all. Rumors were circulating about what was going on in the palace. Everywhere people were gossiping about King Belshazzar and sharing wild stories about the royal family. Servants who worked on the palace grounds in Babylon leaked information that King Nabonidus was in hiding. Even worse, it was said his son King Belshazzar was having one drunken party after another to silence the nagging doubts in his mind about a possible Medo-Persian invasion.

When word came that the city of Sippar to the north had fallen to the

Medes and Persians, everyone really began to worry. Caleb heard about it when he and Tamzi went up to Isi's guard tower on the wall late one afternoon.

"My brother will know the latest," Tamzi told Caleb. "He told me a runner came in just yesterday with news from the north that no one will believe."

The boys raced up the last flight of stairs in record time. "Is it true?" Caleb blurted as he burst into the guard tower.

"Is what true?" Isi said absentmindedly, hardly looking up from his task of stringing bows for military archers.

"That messengers are coming in from Sippar?"

"We've got messengers showing up all the time." Isi handed Caleb a newly strung bow. "Go ahead; try it. See if these aren't the finest bows around."

Caleb held the bow in his left hand and drew the bowstring back with all his might. Cords of leather and plant fibers had been twisted together to make the bowstring strong and resilient.

"So, is that the only reason you came up here, or do you want to help?" Isi grabbed another archer's bow, put one end of it on the floor, stepped on it lightly, and bent it forcefully to string it tight.

"We want to help," Tamzi replied. He glanced at Caleb. "Can you stay for a while?"

"For a short time, but not too long. Uncle Jabez wants me to come home and tread some more clay." Caleb watched Isi string another bow. "Show me how to do that, and I'll stay. That is if Tamzi will come home and help tread clay too."

Tamzi made a face. "OK, I'll help. Not that it's my favorite job in the world."

The boys set to work stringing bows to test them and then unstringing them again, so the strings wouldn't stretch out. All the while they worked, they asked questions.

"What did the military runner from Sippar say? Was there a battle?"

"How many soldiers were there? Was King Cyrus at the battlefield?"

"The army never even fought a battle," Isi said matter-of-factly. "King Nabonidus fled from Sippar, leaving his mercenary army of Lydian soldiers to face the Medes and Persians—more than three hundred thousand of them."

"King Nabonidus fled?" Caleb's jaw dropped. "Where did he go?"

Isi shrugged. "Some say here."

"I heard that, too, just yesterday." Tamzi's eyes lit up. "Everybody was talking about it in the marketplace, but I didn't believe it."

"Who knows?" Isi finished stringing another bow. "All I know is that he left the generals to face King Cyrus alone."

"Really?"

"Yup, the Babylonian generals had to negotiate a deal with King Cyrus and then surrender." Isi lowered his voice and looked this way and that. "I hate to say it, but any king that would act like that and desert his army is a coward. If he's going to keep doing stuff like that, he won't be king much longer. The Medes and Persians will see to that."

Caleb kept stringing bows, but he thought long and hard about what Isi was saying. *Is it possible that King Nabonidus fled from Sippar and the generals had surrendered in shame? The Medes and Persians had won the battle without even fighting?*

Now there was nothing standing between Babylon and its enemy.

Cyrus had conquered the Euphrates and Tigris River valleys, and every major city had fallen to his powerful army. The famous general had conquered the Babylonian army at the Battle of Opis. He had broken through Nebuchadnezzar's famous wall north of Babylon, which was built to keep out the Medes. Now there were no more roadblocks. Sippar had been the last city in the Medo-Persian path to Babylon.

Caleb stood to his feet and looked out across the river valley stretching to the west and north. Babylon was next. King Cyrus would soon come to stake his claim on the capital of the fading Babylonian Empire. There was no doubt in Caleb's mind, and only one question remained unanswered: could Babylon withstand an attack from Cyrus the Great?

Shadows stretched long across the landscape, as Caleb left the guard tower. It would be time for the evening meal soon, but first he had to go home to do his chores. The goats would arrive home soon and would need to be milked. He would have to tread more clay in the kneading trough as well as fire up the kiln for the finished jars and pots. Caleb finished his chores in record time. By the time the sun had set, the family was gathering to eat, and he was ravenous. He had been so busy in the guard tower that afternoon, he had forgotten about food. Now he was so hungry he was tempted to eat before the family had a chance to ask God's blessing on the food.

But Uncle Jabez arrived home from the market in time to save the day. "Blessed are You, oh Lord our God," he prayed, "Master of the universe, who nourishes the whole world in goodness, with grace, kindness, and compassion. He gives bread to all flesh, for His mercy endures forever. Amen."

Caleb reached for the flatbread, tore off a piece, and shoved it in his mouth. Right now he could think of nothing but food.

"I hear we're going to have a special guest coming to the synagogue this Sabbath," Uncle Jabez said.

Aunt Helah set a basket of bitter herbs in the center of the family circle. "What's his name?" she asked.

Uncle Jabez dished himself up a bowl of delicious stew. "I didn't ask," he replied between spoonfuls of lentils and chickpeas.

Caleb continued eating, but the wheels were turning in his head. *What will happen to the Jews if the Medes and Persians conquer Babylon? Most Jews enjoy a good life in Babylon, but we aren't really free. If the Medes and Persians manage to break through the defenses of Babylon, the Jews will become the subjects of the Medo-Persian Empire; that could change a lot of things for us.*

The thought of such a thing scared Caleb. *But what can I do about it? Only God knows what is going to happen.*

13

The Sabbath day finally arrived, and everyone gathered expectantly in the synagogue. A feeling of excitement filled the morning air. Caleb couldn't remember a day quite like it. *Who is the guest coming to worship with us today? Where is he from, and what will he talk about?*

A Levite singer got up to lead the congregation and chose a famous song from the 103rd psalm.

"Bless the LORD, O my soul;
And all that is within me, bless His holy name!
Bless the LORD, O my soul,
And forget not all His benefits:
Who forgives all your iniquities,
Who heals all your diseases,
Who redeems your life from destruction,
Who crowns you with loving kindness and tender mercies,
Who satisfies your mouth with good things,
So that your youth is renewed like the eagle's" (verses 1–5).

Caleb enjoyed singing more than anything, and that psalm really hit the spot on a morning like this.

Zaccai the scribe got up to make a few announcements. He welcomed everyone and then took a scroll out of the cabinet at the front of the synagogue. He read,

"A good name is to be chosen rather than great riches,
Loving favor rather than silver and gold.
The rich and the poor have this in common,
The LORD is the Maker of them all. . . .
By humility and the fear of the LORD
Are riches and honor and life" (Proverbs 22:1, 2, 4).

Suddenly, the door to the synagogue opened and in walked a distinguished old man with two attendants. A buzz of voices swept the room as the guest found a place near the front and sat down. *Who is this visitor?* Caleb wondered, leaning forward with interest, but he didn't have long to wait.

"We're honored to have the prophet Daniel with us today," Zaccai said, nodding at the guest. "He has been a champion for us in the Babylonian court and received many visions from the Lord our God."

"Wow!" Caleb gasped. So this was the prophet Daniel, the famous man the beggar at the canal had spoken of and the prophet Uncle Jabez had told stories about! He had heard so much about this holy man and had wanted to meet him for such a long time. Now that day had come, and it was just about the biggest day Caleb could remember in the synagogue.

What will his message be today? Will he talk about his early days in Babylon? Will he share any of his visions? Will he talk about the Medo-Persian army on the march?

"Peace be to you," Daniel greeted the worshipers and then invited God's blessing on the congregation. The prophet was an old man, well advanced in years, but his back was straight, and his head held high. He wore a turban, as was the tradition of the Jews while in the synagogue, and had a short-cropped beard, which was as white as snow.

He unrolled a large scroll he had brought with him and began to read from it:

"For thus says the LORD: After seventy years are completed at Babylon, I will visit you and perform My good word toward you, and cause you to return to this place. For I know the thoughts that I think toward you, says the LORD, thoughts of peace and not of evil, to give you a future and a hope. Then you will call upon Me and go and pray to Me, and I will listen to you. And you will seek Me and find Me, when you search for Me with all your heart. I will be found by you, says the LORD, and I will bring you back from your captivity; I will gather you from all the nations and from all the places where I have driven you, says the LORD, and I will bring you to the place from which I cause you to be carried away captive" (Jeremiah 29:10–14).

Caleb's jaw dropped. *This is the prophet Jeremiah's seventy-year prophecy about the return of the Jews to the Holy Land! It is exactly what the scribe Zaccai talked about in the Sabbath service several weeks before. It is the message many people in the synagogue doubt will be fulfilled. Even Grandpa Obed said it will never come!*

Caleb felt a rush of energy. *Others might doubt the Word of the Lord, but there is no hesitation on Daniel's part. He speaks with confidence and authority as if he really believes the prophecy. And why wouldn't he?* Caleb thought. *He is a prophet. If God tells him something is going to happen, it will happen. Can't everyone believe that?* Caleb was so excited he could hardly sit still on his mat. *Jeremiah said it, and now the prophet Daniel is saying it too. It is nearly time for God's people to go home!*

"But that's not all," Daniel said with conviction. "There's more. Jeremiah also speaks of what Babylon can expect when this prophecy is fulfilled." He unrolled the scroll a bit more to read another passage.

" ' "Then it will come to pass," ' " Daniel read, " ' "when seventy years are completed, that I will punish the king of Babylon and that nation, the land of the Chaldeans, for their iniquity," ' says the LORD; ' "and I will make it a perpetual desolation. So I will bring on that land all My words which I have pronounced against it, all that is written in this book, which Jeremiah has prophesied concerning all the nations" ' " (Jeremiah 25:12, 13).

"Jehovah is a God of love, but He also represents justice," Daniel added. "There comes a day when He can no longer accept the wicked ways of His people and their desecration of His holy commandments." Daniel bowed his head. "That's us, exactly. We know how evil our people had become when God allowed us to be hauled away in chains to Babylon. And we paid for it."

He raised his hands toward heaven. "And Jehovah expects as much from our enemies. They may not know Jehovah as we do, but there comes a judgment day for them just as surely as it comes for us. And it will come, for the mouth of the Lord has spoken it."

Caleb was surprised that Daniel would say such harsh things about the kingdom of Babylon, even if he was quoting from the prophet Jeremiah. He had come as a prisoner to this land. He had been privileged to work for the Babylonian government for many years.

Won't he get in trouble for saying things like this?

But Caleb guessed Daniel knew what he was doing. He was an expert on the laws of the land. He knew exactly what he could and couldn't say about Babylon, and they weren't really his words anyway. They were the words of Jeremiah, the famous prophet of doom.

The service ended, and everyone just sat there in solemn reverence, as if waiting for the prophet to say something more. Then they began to get up one by one, until the synagogue was nearly empty.

Caleb remained a while longer, wishing the prophet had talked longer. Though he had finally seen the great man of God, he felt a need for something more. With all his heart, he wished he could talk to the great Jewish statesman, but he was just a boy. Why would Daniel, the prophet of the Lord, be interested in talking to him?

14

On the way home from the synagogue's worship service, Caleb talked with his grandpa about everything Daniel had said. "Do you really think the prophecy of Jeremiah is going to be fulfilled?" Caleb asked excitedly.

"Which one?" Grandpa Obed asked. "The one about us returning home, or the one about Babylon being punished for the horrible things it did to God's people?"

Caleb shrugged. "Why not both? If the people of Babylon are wicked, why shouldn't they have to answer to God too? Maybe they deserve it like we did."

Grandpa swatted at a fly buzzing around his face. "Oh, there's no doubt about that. The Babylonians are like the Assyrians, who were some of the cruelest and most bloodthirsty people who ever walked the face of the earth. As to the Babylonians letting us go home to Judah? I don't think so. Why would they bring us here, only to let us go back home? Besides that, we've helped make Babylon rich with our shrewd business skills. We pay our taxes. We buy and trade and sell just like everyone, except we do it better than the Babylonians. No doubt about it. The thousands of Jews living in the Euphrates and Tigris River valleys have brought a lot of wealth to Babylon."

"But God promised we would get to return!" Caleb argued. "If He told Jeremiah these things would happen, then He's got to keep His promise."

"Well, yes and no." Grandpa Obed looked doubtful. "Remember, sometimes prophecies are conditional."

Caleb felt a little frustrated that Grandpa Obed was trying so hard to be difficult. "All right then, what about the prophet Daniel?" he said, looking for ammunition to make his point. "He didn't say anything about a conditional prophecy today. It seemed pretty clear to him."

Grandpa nodded. "Can't argue with you there, Son."

"Well then, what's the problem?" Caleb stared at Grandpa Obed in surprise. "If you ask me, I think a lot of these prophecies have to do with us. Do we want them to be fulfilled? Do we want them to come to pass? Maybe we should be praying to God and telling Him what we want."

"Whoa there, Son." Grandpa Obed put his hand on Caleb's shoulder as if to restrain him. "We don't tell God what to do! He tells us what will be."

Caleb squinted up at his grandpa. "Yes, sir. I'm not trying to be rude, but I was thinking about the story of Sodom and Gomorrah. Those cities were going to be destroyed for certain, but Abraham prayed that God would save Lot and his family. And He did. Then there's the story of Joshua," Caleb hurried on. "He was winning a battle, but the sun was about to go down and he needed more time. So he prayed that God would make the sun stay up longer to let him finish the battle."

"And God answered his prayer." Grandpa Obed made a face. "OK, you got me again, Son."

"So you see, Grandpa, I was thinking maybe God wants us to pray more than whine about what we think is coming. We should accept Him at His word. He wants what is best for us, not the other way around."

Grandpa Obed snorted in disbelief. "You surprise me sometimes, Caleb, you know that?"

Late that afternoon Tamzi came over and ate the evening meal with Caleb and his family. Saarah's friend Jemi was there, too, and everyone was having fun, laughing and talking. Daniel's words that day had lifted their spirits, it seemed.

Caleb watched Jemi out of the corner of his eye. She was pretty, with dark hair and dimples that danced on her face when she laughed. Once she caught him staring at her, but he blushed and turned quickly away.

Everyone was talking about Daniel's visit to the synagogue. The conversation went round and round, mostly between Uncle Jabez and Grandpa Obed. Caleb was fourteen, but boys weren't supposed to talk much at a meal. That would come later when they were grown men and considered adults at the age of twenty-one. For now, they had to spend most of their time listening.

After the meal, the two boys went up on the roof to do some stargazing. "I saw you looking at Jemi," Tamzi teased. "You like her, don't you?"

"Maybe; what if I do?" Caleb blushed again, but it was dark up on the roof, so he hoped Tamzi wouldn't notice. "Jemi's pretty and really nice too."

"Can't argue with you there," Tamzi grinned.

The evening was young, and the boys fell silent as they searched the sky for the Great Bear constellation, the Scorpion, and the Bull. The moon was rising in the east, and the nighthawks had come out to swoop in their search for an evening meal of insects.

Caleb also told Tamzi about Daniel's visit to the synagogue and his words about the prophet Jeremiah's prophecies.

Tamzi's eyes grew big at the news. "Does that mean you and your family might leave and go back to the country your ancestors came from?"

"I think so, but my grandfather doesn't. I heard him say he doesn't even want to leave Babylon."

"Oh. Well, what will you do? You can't break up the family."

"No, we don't want to do that, but really we haven't even talked about that part. I mean, no one has told us we can go. I want to go, I think, but the king hasn't made a law or decree telling us we can. Actually, I can't imagine that ever happening. Can you?"

Tamzi looked at Caleb with a strange look on his face. "King Belshazzar? Uh, probably not. Why would he? He cares about no one but himself." Tamzi laughed. "I guess he gets to do whatever he wants. He's the king, right?"

"Yeah, for sure." Caleb wanted to laugh, too, but he didn't. "My uncle told me Belshazzar's father, King Nabonidus, was never interested in running Babylon, which is why he put Belshazzar on the throne and told him he could make all the decisions on his own." Caleb shook his head. "We don't need to worry about my family breaking up. It's not likely the Babylonian government will ever let us go back to Judah anyway."

"So then, what will you do with that prophecy from your prophet, that Daniel guy?"

"And Jeremiah."

"Yeah, him too."

"I don't know."

"If you're not going to go back to Judah, what then?"

Caleb didn't know what to say, but he gave it one last shot. "In that case, I guess God's going to have to work it out." He stared at Tamzi. "I believe in the prophecies. If you had heard the prophet talk today in the synagogue, you would know what I'm talking about. He was so convincing!"

Tamzi went home late that night, but the next morning he was back. "My father needs help again at the royal warehouse," he said. "He's asking if you want to come help."

15

Y ou don't have classes today, so you can go once your chores are done," Uncle Jabez said, "but make sure you're actually helping Tamzi's father. I don't want you going just so you can play games at the warehouse."

"Yes, sir," Caleb said politely.

"Oh, and Caleb, see if you can find out any more about those crates from Judah. I know it's a long shot, but the whole thing has got me thinking."

Caleb grinned at his uncle. "You're kidding," he said with a twinkle in his eye. "I'm way ahead of you, sir."

The goats were already milked and gone for the day with the herd boy. All that remained for the boys to do was empty the kiln of clay pots and jars and load them on the donkey cart. In record time, they helped Grandpa Obed get the pottery to the market and then it was off to the warehouse.

When they arrived, they found Malik already supervising the workers in the main warehouse. After a quick hello, the boys helped unload a shipment of exquisite furniture from Egypt, which had arrived several months before. "Thanks for coming," Malik told the boys. "We never have enough workers here at the warehouse to help unpack all the stuff our armies have brought in."

Caleb stared at the beautiful furniture being unpacked. He hadn't known there were such fine things in the world, and his eyes grew big at each new item they took out of the crates. The furniture had been wrapped in heavy linen. When the boys helped unwind the long, white strips of cloth, it was plain to see why Egypt was such a famous place.

Long, low tables of black ebony gleamed in the morning light streaming through the warehouse windows up near the ceiling. Caleb thought the tables looked almost like glass—shiny and hard to the touch.

Tall, narrow vanities of almug wood, with slender legs, were lifted out, and the workers had to be especially careful not to damage them. Caleb couldn't stop staring at the fine artwork etched up and down the legs of the furniture. There were carvings of serpents and foxes and ibis and crocodiles. The carvings were good likenesses of animals and birds, but Caleb knew they were supposed to represent the pagan gods of Egypt.

When he thought about that, it kind of made him sad. The Egyptians probably had the smartest civilization since Noah's flood, but what a waste. They were so wrapped up in the worship of creatures that they couldn't stop long enough to recognize the Creator who had made the creatures.

Once the most powerful empire in the world, Egypt was now a conquered nation. None of the pharaohs had been able to stand against the attacks of the ferocious Assyrians, and they had been no match for the Babylonians either. Nebuchadnezzar and his father, Nabopolassar, had conquered the people of the pyramids, bending them until they finally broke like a reed in the wind.

"Has-beens," is what Grandpa Obed always called the Egyptians. "Relics of the past. A nation of corrupt worshipers is what they are, trying to tap into the dark powers of the supernatural world."

All morning the boys helped open crates and take inventory of what was in them. After a quick lunch of barley gruel, the boys were sent off to work in the chamber where they had worked the last time Caleb had come.

A score of crates from Arabia were open in the middle of the floor but still packed, and the boys set about taking inventory of the items.

They found ornate chests made of acacia wood, decorated with rubies, diamonds, and other precious jewels. In another crate, they found boxes of all sizes made of camel skin and adorned with pearls. In yet another crate, they unpacked items made of hand-carved ivory, which was as white as snow.

During a break, Caleb and Tamzi climbed up on the stacks of crates to have another look at the marked cartons of relics from Judah. The wooden crates were still there and still unopened. Caleb heaved a sigh of relief, knowing that they had not been disturbed or taken away.

But were the contents of the crates actually artifacts from the kingdom of Judah? Did the wooden boxes contain the ancient artifacts the writing claimed were inside? And, what did they look like?

"I wish we could open the crates and see what's in them," Caleb said wistfully. "It's all I've been thinking about since we first saw the crates. The suspense is driving me crazy! Do you think we could just take a little peak?"

"Better not." Tamzi shook his head. "See that red plaster patch there on the edge of the crate? It's a royal seal. There's one on the other side, too, and no one can break them unless he has authority from the king."

"Like who? Your father?"

"Yeah, my father would be able to do it or some other high official from the royal court." Tamzi nodded. "But don't get your hopes up, Caleb. There's a pretty good chance the things from Judah are already gone."

"But the seal is still there, unbroken," Caleb insisted. "Wouldn't that mean the original relics are still in there?"

"Not necessarily." Tamzi squinted at the crates with the writing on them. "They may have repacked the crates with items they want to send off somewhere else in the kingdom. They do that sort of thing all the time. A few weeks ago my father packed up some crates with stuff for the king of Tyre. He put a seal on the crates just like the ones on these crates."

Caleb's heart sank. Tamzi was probably right. The chances of actually finding the lost treasures here in this warehouse were probably pretty slim. When King Nebuchadnezzar brought the temple treasures to Babylon almost seventy years ago, his officials probably unpacked them right away. They probably put them in the temples of their famous gods.

In Nebuchadnezzar's mind, this would make the Babylonian temples even more holy than they already were. And, of course, putting Judah's captured relics in his own temples and shrines would have shown King Nebuchadnezzar's superiority over the Jews and the God they worshiped.

The whole thing made Caleb want to cringe and reminded him why the precious treasures had ended up in Babylon in the first place. Judah had been unfaithful to Jehovah and had broken their ancient covenant with Him. The nation had apostatized. They had worshiped idols, been sexually immoral, and sacrificed their children to pagan gods. They had robbed the poor and shed innocent blood in the courts of their land. All these wicked deeds had cost Caleb's people the golden temple with God's holy treasures, and the kingdom of Judah was no more. It had vanished like the dew on the grass at sunrise.

The thought of it all made Caleb feel sick inside. Then he thought of something. *Maybe the prophet Daniel can help. At one time, he was a powerful officer in the Babylonian court. But that was years ago. Is he still a man of influence in government affairs?* Caleb tried to remember if Zaccai the scribe or Allamu the blind beggar had said anything about that, and his heart raced at the idea.

Of course, there was always the chance that Daniel wouldn't want to get involved. If he was no longer handling business in the royal court, he might turn down the chance to help.

But there was another problem. Caleb didn't even know where Daniel lived. He didn't have a clue. *How can I ever find him, even if I did have the courage to ask for his help?* He could always get Uncle Jabez to help him find Daniel, but he was afraid to ask for fear his uncle would say he shouldn't bother the man of God.

16

The more Caleb thought about it, the more he was sure the prophet Daniel was his man. The wooden crates with the writing on them were still sealed in the warehouse, and only someone with authority could open them. Daniel might be that person; one could always hope.

But how can I find Daniel? Where does he live? Then Caleb thought of something. *Maybe Daniel will come to the synagogue again for Sabbath services sometime.* The prophet was a faithful Jew, so Caleb figured he must be a worshiper with Jews at another location. What he needed to do was find all the other synagogues in Babylon.

He would go in search of Daniel. He would find the place where he worshiped and go to meet the prophet, if he had the nerve. As he planned, the fact that Daniel didn't even know who Caleb was never occurred to him.

As it turned out, his plans never got that far. Imagine his surprise the next Sabbath to see the prophet come again to worship in the synagogue where Caleb and his family worshiped! When Daniel walked through the door, Caleb knew he had to talk to him. Seeing the prophet again was like an answered prayer.

After the service was over, Caleb jumped up from his place on the men's side and hurried to where Daniel was sitting. It was now or never. If he didn't find the courage to speak to Daniel while the prophet was visiting the synagogue, it might never happen at all. However, as he got close to the prophet, he suddenly lost his nerve. Daniel was an important man. Caleb felt tongue-tied and jittery, and there seemed to be a loud ringing in his ears.

What is happening? Caleb wondered. As he stared down at the prophet sitting cross-legged on the floor, he realized this was his moment and he was letting it slip away. He opened his mouth to speak, but nothing came out.

Then Zaccai the scribe suddenly appeared, coming to Caleb's rescue. "Your Honor," he said, bowing respectfully to Daniel. "This is Caleb, a nephew of Jabez, son of Obed. Their family worships with us every week. He was here the other Sabbath when you came to speak." The scribe put his hand on the boy's shoulder. "I believe he would like a word with you."

"Ah, yes." The prophet smiled up at Caleb. "What can I do for you, my son?"

Caleb suddenly snapped out of his mental fog and came to his senses. The prophet Daniel was looking up at him, waiting for an answer.

"Please, sir," Caleb began, "there's something very important I need to talk to you about." He hesitated and then hurried on. "I was in the warehouse of the royal archives the other day, working with a friend whose father manages the warehouse. While there, we discovered something we think might be very important for the Jewish people."

Daniel studied Caleb's face with keen interest, waiting for the boy to go on. Caleb shook his head instead and bent down to whisper something in his ear.

The prophet nodded slowly, and his eyes lit up. "*Hmm*, that sounds very interesting. Why don't you and your uncle come to my apartment suite later this evening? We can talk more then," he said.

Caleb's eyes nearly popped out of his head at the invitation. This was unbelievable! He had wished more than anything to talk with the holy man of God; never in his wildest dreams had he thought Daniel would be interested in what a boy had to say! But to be invited to visit the prophet in his own private home? This whole thing was turning out to be more exciting than Caleb would have thought possible. He had a good imagination, but he knew it hadn't included this scenario.

When Uncle Jabez saw Caleb talking with Daniel, he ambled over and joined them for the end of the conversation. "The prophet has invited us to see him later today in his home," Caleb told his uncle excitedly.

"Really? What's the occasion?" Uncle Jabez glanced at Caleb and then at the prophet Daniel.

"You've got a sharp nephew," Daniel said, giving Uncle Jabez a wink.

Uncle Jabez looked confused, but then a glimmer of recognition slowly crossed his face. "Is this what I think it is?" he asked, squinting at Caleb.

"Come to my house after the Sabbath hours, and you can tell me everything," Daniel nodded knowingly.

Caleb left the synagogue with his uncle and grandfather, but he was gliding on air. All the way home Grandpa Obed kept asking what the conversation between Caleb and Daniel had been about, but Uncle Jabez gave him little more than a smile.

The afternoon dragged slowly by, and Caleb was sure he would burst from the excitement of what was coming. He had to admit that he had never spent the Sabbath hours wishing the time would pass more quickly.

But the time did pass, and the hour finally arrived for Caleb and Uncle Jabez to leave for their appointment. The sun had set already. The family prayers had been said. Verses of Scripture had been read from a scroll that was taken from its shelf in the great room just off the family courtyard.

As they passed through the streets of Babylon, which were now growing dark with the evening twilight, Caleb and Uncle Jabez talked. All the way there they discussed what they would say when they arrived at Daniel's home for the visit, but mostly they wondered what he would have to say about the crates in the warehouse.

Would he believe them? Would he have some inside information about the case of the mysterious crates? Would he be interested enough to help them investigate?

As they neared the district where Daniel lived, Caleb got more and more nervous. This part of the city was much nicer than where he and his family lived. In fact, it was much nicer than any place he had ever been.

"This is the district where government officials such as Daniel live,"

Uncle Jabez said quietly. "They have been the most powerful people in the world for years. Serving the king of Babylon is no small accomplishment. It's no wonder everybody here lives like kings themselves."

And live like kings they did. High walls of sun-dried brick, covered with white plaster, lined the villas bordering the streets, and Caleb could see the fancy homes towering up behind the walls. Through open gates, he sometimes got glimpses of the bright lights in the homes and the sumptuous patio gardens. Lamps lined the flowered walkways, and giddy music was wafting out on the evening air. He could smell wonderful foods being prepared, and there was laughter.

"I had no idea," was all Caleb could say, but it was enough. To speak at a time like this seemed silly. Far better to drink it all in and remember it for what it was—a place he would never live and a life he would never lead.

17

Finding Daniel's home was easy enough. The prophet's directions had been very clear. At the gates of the government complex where he lived, Caleb and Uncle Jabez told the guard Daniel was expecting them for a visit. The guard nodded politely, then escorted them up a wide avenue that approached the gates of the palace itself. From there, it was off the main street and down a walkway lined with gardens to Daniel's suite of rooms.

Uncle Jabez rang a little tinkling bell at Daniel's gate, and within a few moments, a well-dressed servant answered the call. Without a word, he quickly ushered Caleb and his uncle into the presence of the old prophet.

"Welcome, my friends. Peace be to you," Daniel said. "Why don't you sit down here, and my attendants will offer you some refreshment?" He smiled kindly and gestured toward some padded benches in the main room.

Uncle Jabez gave a slight bow, and Caleb followed his example as they sat down. Another servant suddenly appeared with a towel and a basin of water to wash their dusty feet; shortly thereafter a third servant arrived with a platter of things to eat. Caleb sampled the sweet cakes and slices of melon and sipped some apricot nectar.

This is the life, he thought as he gazed around him at the accommodations of Daniel's suite. The furnishings were few, though much more extravagant than anything Caleb was used to. He had been to the homes of some prosperous Jewish merchants, but Daniel's apartments easily rivaled them.

Under Caleb's feet lay a plush Persian carpet. Ornate tables with short legs sat in every corner, along with unusual-looking chairs that had obviously been imported from the north. Gorgeous, colorful tapestries decorated the walls, and long drapes of purple satin hung at the openings of doors and windows. Even more impressive to Caleb was the torch-lit fountain that bubbled just outside the main window in an open courtyard.

"Government accommodations for royal officials," Daniel said with a humble nod of his head as he saw Caleb glancing around at the fine furnishings. "Not something I would choose for myself," he added quickly.

"I trust you had a blessed Sabbath day," he said. "It's always a welcome relief at the end of a busy week. Now, let's hear about your 'amazing find.' Tell me all about it," he said with a warm smile that helped Caleb relax.

Uncle Jabez glanced at Caleb. "Well, I think my nephew should do most of the talking. He's the one who made the discovery."

The prophet turned to Caleb. "All right, Caleb, give me the details."

"It's been a few days now," Caleb began. "A few weeks, I guess. We had been working for my friend's father, Malik, son of Gudea. He's the director and supervisor at the warehouse of the royal archives off the main thoroughfare, where the army and royal dignitaries parade on feast days. Anyway, we were working in one of the large storerooms of the warehouse when I happened to see some crates with writing on them that described what was inside. Some of them said, 'War trophies from Judah.' Others said things such as, 'Relics from Zedekiah's temple,' and 'Temple treasures from Jerusalem.' "

"*Hmm,* that does sound like a discovery." Daniel studied Caleb's face. "Of course, the crates might not actually have those things in them anymore, but then again, they might. My first thought is that the king's officials may have opened those crates long ago in the days of King

Nebuchadnezzar—probably when he first brought them here from Judah."

"That's what we were thinking," Uncle Jabez admitted, "but we don't know anyone with real authority, other than you and Malik, and Malik is a Babylonian. We were hoping you could help us find out before Malik opens them up himself. It's clear he has no clue as to their real importance."

"Well, I would not say I have much authority anymore. I haven't served in the royal court for years. King Nabonidus did call for me a few times after King Nebuchadnezzar died but less and less frequently down through the years.

"So Caleb, what exactly do you guess is in those crates?" Daniel asked, changing the subject. "You saw what was written on them. Do you think the inscriptions are telling us what is really inside?"

"The temple treasures, maybe; the idols of gold and silver, no. Like you said, it's hard to believe they would have left the gold and silver idols of Judah in the crates. We figured Nebuchadnezzar would have taken them and put them in his temples and then later even melted them down for the precious metal they're made of. They're not gods I'd be proud of." Caleb made a face. "We have only one God, but Nebuchadnezzar didn't know that. In the days following Judah's captivity, he didn't know the power of Jehovah."

Daniel gave Caleb a wide grin. "You're a smart fellow, Son. The Lord did give King Nebuchadnezzar plenty of opportunities to learn from those of us who honored Jehovah. My friends Hananiah, Mishael, Azariah, and I stood up for God on several occasions. I'm sure you've heard some of those stories."

"The food you wouldn't eat in the king's school. I know about that," Caleb said. "The story about the king's dream of the image and how you helped interpret his dream and the real image he made of gold—the huge one on the Plain of Dura."

"It's been a long time," Daniel sighed. "I was so proud of my friends. Nothing could make them dishonor Jehovah, not even a burning furnace. Of course, that gave King Nebuchadnezzar a real jolt. He wasn't used to people challenging his authority like that."

"And the most amazing story of all?" Daniel's face turned serious. "God had to turn my good friend Nebuchadnezzar into an animal before he would accept Jehovah as Lord of heaven and earth. He became a raging beast, and I had to live through that.

"So, if idols of gold and silver aren't in those crates, what is?" Daniel changed the subject again.

Caleb shook his head. "I wouldn't know. I don't even know what was in Solomon's temple before it was destroyed. I've lived in Babylon my whole life."

"*Hmm.* Well, I know what some of the items in those crates might be, if they haven't already been melted down for their value in gold and silver. I saw lots of things carried out of the house of God that terrible day nearly seventy years ago." Daniel frowned. "It was hard to watch. Ours was the first deportation to Babylon almost twenty years before the final destruction of Jerusalem. I was just a young man at the time and didn't see everything they took, but I'm told they left the larger pieces of furniture in the temple. I did see them loading up lots of other stuff in the wagons—golden bowls and cups, silver candlesticks, gold and silver pans and platters and basins and knives. If anything is in those crates, I'd expect it to be those kinds of things."

"Would you be willing to come to the warehouse one day to inspect the vessels for yourself?" Uncle Jabez asked. "I think that's our best chance right now at sorting this thing out."

Daniel nodded. "I could do that. When shall I come?"

"If Caleb can manage to get permission to work there with Tamzi tomorrow, that would be our best bet, I think." Uncle Jabez put a hand on Caleb's shoulder. "Malik knows him, and he'd be there to show you where the crates are exactly."

Caleb could hardly sleep that night in anticipation of the excitement he knew was coming on the morrow. He was up before dawn, earlier than usual, to see that his chores were done. He didn't want anything to hold him up if Tamzi should ask him to come to the warehouse to work again.

But Tamzi didn't come. All that morning Caleb waited, and the suspense was killing him! And then, while they were eating their midday meal of lentil stew and flatbread, Tamzi finally did show up.

"Caleb," he shouted excitedly, "my pa says you can come to work with me again today at the warehouse, if you want." Caleb didn't need a second invitation. Off he raced with Tamzi, not even bothering to finish his meal.

When they arrived at the warehouse, he got right to work helping Tamzi unpack and repack some crates in the main warehouse. "Why are we packing up these crates?" Caleb asked Tamzi.

"My father says we don't have enough space in the warehouse for all the stuff that's stored here, so we're repacking them to make more room."

Caleb tried to focus on the work at hand, but all he could think about was the crates in the other storeroom. *Are the markings on the crates authentic, showing what is actually inside them? Are the treasures of Judah's ancient kingdom in that room? Will Daniel actually show up to help us find out?*

18

Halfway through the afternoon Daniel showed up at the warehouse, just as planned. He asked to see the crates from Judah, and again Caleb climbed up to show him and Malik where they were.

"Ah, yes; those are the crates you discovered the other day?" Malik asked. "From Judah, aren't they?"

"Would it be possible for us to bring the crates down here?" Daniel asked. Obviously at the age of eighty-five, he would be unable to climb up where the wooden boxes were stacked near the ceiling.

A dozen workers were brought in to help lift the heavy crates, and soon the place was humming like a beehive. The men carefully carried the crates down the stairs of stacked boxes. One by one they came down, the heavier ones were smaller, and the lighter ones much larger than the rest.

When the floor was littered with crates of many sizes, the workers left. Only Daniel and Malik remained behind with the boys in the chamber.

"Which one first?" Malik asked, scanning the crates.

Daniel laid his hand on a crate larger than the rest. "This one," he said. On the crate in faded letters was written "War trophies from Judah."

The wooden boards were old. The royal red plaster seals were still on the crate and also looked to be very old indeed.

Malik forced a pry bar under the lid of the crate and wrenched it loose. The lid fell away, throwing a cloud of dust in the air, making everyone wheeze and choke. Daniel cleared the air with a wave of his hand and then reached inside the crate to remove an item. The others watched as he carefully unwound old linen rags from the object, revealing an exquisite vase made of ivory. The artwork on the vase revealed elaborate flowers and pomegranates from top to bottom. Bundle after bundle was then removed from the crate, all of them wrapped in the old linen strips, which were yellow and disintegrating with age. The bundles revealed boxes, idols, jars, musical instruments, and decorative panels, all carved out of ivory.

Caleb was a little disappointed at the contents of the crate. The ivory artifacts were nice, but they weren't the gold and silver treasures from the temple. A second large crate was opened, this one revealing scores of hand-carved wooden objects. Inside were good-luck charms, fine lattice panels, and ebony chests with inlaid mother-of-pearl. There were also idols of stone and wood in the crate: some were short, fat, and ugly, while others were elegant with smooth polished surfaces.

It appeared that most of the crates had never been disturbed, but was this all they contained? The relics appeared to be genuine enough. They were wonderful pieces of artwork, indeed from the lost kingdom of ancient Judah. However, they were definitely not treasures of gold and silver from Solomon's temple.

Caleb didn't know what to think. He was sure he remembered seeing crates that specifically mentioned temple treasures inside them. One even had Zedekiah's name on it. *Where is that crate?* He climbed over the crates, searching here and there, turning the smaller ones around and around on the warehouse floor.

Then he found it sitting by itself at one end of the warehouse floor. "Relics from Zedekiah's temple," the Aramaic writing said on one end of the crate.

"Can we open this one over here?" Caleb called. "I bet we'll find what we're looking for in this crate."

Malik came with his pry bar and wrenched that lid free, too, and what a surprise awaited them! Inside they found the precious treasures they had been looking for: fine golden bowls and goblets, elaborately designed, and no two alike.

Another crate sitting nearby held pans and basins and shovels made of silver. A third crate, larger than the previous two, held golden platters and silver basins.

"There's no doubt about it," the prophet Daniel said confidently. "These are the ancient vessels from our holy temple in Jerusalem. I actually remember seeing some of them when I was just a boy." He turned to Malik. "The great King Nebuchadnezzar confiscated them and brought them here to Babylon, but they rightfully belong to Jehovah, the Creator of heaven and earth."

Malik bowed respectfully to the prophet. "What shall we do with them?" he asked.

"What can we do?" Daniel picked up one of the golden vessels to examine it and then put it back in the crate. "These vessels are really under the control of the royal steward. Let's wait and see what the Lord has in mind."

Caleb was excited beyond words. They had wanted to find the original artifacts of gold and silver stolen from Judah's temple storehouses so long ago, and now they had done it! They had accomplished what they came for. The temple treasures had been in the warehouse the whole time. Finding the ancient artifacts was like a dream come true!

The afternoon adventure ended, but Daniel didn't look as pleased as Caleb thought he would be. In fact, he seemed disturbed as he left the warehouse. His shoulders slumped a little, and his head was down.

Caleb was worried about Daniel. The next day he thought about the holy man of God and his reaction when they opened the crates full of treasures. *Why did he look so sad when he left the warehouse after such an incredible discovery? Isn't he glad to find the temple treasures? Doesn't he realize what this might mean for God's people? Or is there something else bothering him that he doesn't want to talk about?*

The following morning a messenger came to Caleb's house, asking that Caleb and his uncle come to Daniel's private quarters again. "Master Daniel is asking that you share the evening meal with him," said the servant. "He will expect you at the twelfth hour."

All day Caleb wondered what the prophet might want. *Is it something about the temple treasures? Does it have something to do with Daniel's reaction as he left the warehouse that day?*

Caleb and his uncle arrived at Daniel's house as planned and enjoyed the meal just as Caleb imagined he would. Servants served them simple but sumptuous food. For starters, there was an appetizer platter of cucumbers, chickpeas, and garden greens. Next came bowls of savory stew made from lentils and oats, seasoned with leeks, garlic, and chives. A sweet cake topped with *leben* and a tart cherry sauce finished the meal.

After supper, they went to the prophet's study where they sat down on camel-skin hassocks to enjoy the warm evening breezes that blew in from the west. Daniel thanked Caleb for the part he had played in the discovery of Judah's sacred treasures and for his uncle's support in allowing Caleb time at the warehouse.

"Many Jews would be depressed at such a find," Daniel said. "Especially when it involves the looted treasures of the long-forgotten kingdom of Judah. I suppose we should be all the happier for the amazing discovery, but the whole thing has troubled me more than you know."

Daniel gave a heavy sigh, and Caleb now knew he had been right about the prophet. The holy man was greatly disturbed about something, and if Caleb didn't miss his guess, they were about to get to the bottom of it.

"I have something I think you two would be interested in," he said as he stood to his feet and moved to a table where several scrolls lay partly unrolled. "What I have written here are the details of some prophetic visions and dreams God has given me." He tapped the scroll lying on the table with conviction in his eyes.

"I have been shown that Babylon's empire is about to end. It will surely fall, and King Belshazzar is the biggest reason why. His wickedness and lazy ways have condemned the future of his people. Clearly, he has squandered the kingdom his grandfather Nebuchadnezzar worked so hard to build."

"How will it end?" Caleb blurted, suddenly forgetting his manners.

Daniel studied Caleb's face as if trying to decide whether the boy could handle the news.

"Cyrus the Great!" Caleb almost gasped. "The end will come when his Medo-Persian armies surround Babylon!"

"Media-Persia? Ah, yes," the old prophet nodded. "That is the question of the century." He glanced at Caleb and Uncle Jabez and then out the window toward the west. "The Lord God is about to show His hand again. He removes kings and raises up kings. After Babylon will arise another kingdom, inferior, but far more powerful and wealthy. This kingdom will be as ferocious as a bear, able to crush every nation in its path. It will come just as King Nebuchadnezzar's dream said it would so long ago. And it will come in our lifetimes. Even mine, as old as I am," he added quietly.

Daniel put a hand of blessing on Caleb's head. "God is about to do great things," the prophet said prayerfully, "and you, young man, will see it firsthand."

19

Caleb's mind was in a whirl. *I am going to be part of something special. The prophet Daniel says so, but what does he mean by that? What is coming? Does it have anything to do with the prophecies found in the prophet's scroll? Is it connected somehow with the coming of the Medes and the Persians? What about the mysterious prophecies of Jeremiah from so long ago? Do Daniel's predictions of judgment have anything to do with the discovery of the holy relics found in the royal warehouse?* Caleb wanted to know in the worst way but was afraid to ask. There was already too much to think about.

The hour was late. As Caleb and Uncle Jabez left the palace grounds, Daniel handed Uncle Jabez a small clay tablet. "This is a pass should you need to reach me," he said. "I'm available any time, day or night."

It was hard to fall asleep that night when they reached home. Caleb lay on his sleeping mat, but he couldn't escape the thought that something big was about to happen. The prophet Daniel had said it in so many words. He hadn't spelled it out exactly, but that was OK. It was as if he was warning those who had ears to listen.

The next morning Caleb awoke to a commotion in the street. People were running and shouting, but there was so much noise it was hard to make out clearly what anyone was saying.

Caleb jumped up from his sleeping mat and ran up the brick stairway leading to the rooftop. The roof would be a good place to get a view of what was happening in the streets of Babylon. As he stood at the parapet along the edge of the roof, he could see the city was in pandemonium. Men were running down the main boulevards and thoroughfares of Babylon. Merchants and caravan drivers were pulling on donkeys and camels loaded with bundles of goods. Women were crying, and children stood wide-eyed, watching it all.

When Caleb saw Tamzi coming down the street toward his house, he knew the news must be big. And it was. His friend ran through the gate into their courtyard, shouting at the top of his lungs, "The Medo-Persian army is approaching from the west! King Cyrus has finally come!"

The boys raced down the street to climb the nearest staircase on the city wall and have a look. Squadrons of soldiers climbing the stairs blocked their way, but Caleb and Tamzi finally reached the top.

When they arrived at Tamzi's brother's guard tower, they saw a sight to the north that almost made their hearts stop. A long, dark line could be seen stretching out across the blue horizon.

Officers ordered the war engines to be prepared for an attack. Catapults and ballistas were set up on their platforms to face the enemy. The catapults and spear-throwers were set to the correct angle to reach the farthest range possible.

The soldiers were talking excitedly. Archers and spearmen ran to their posts of duty on the wall. The spearmen wore decorative helmets; chest armor made with metal plates fastened together; leather leggings; and colorful kilts, with gold and red tassels hanging from them. Their shields were made of wood or wicker and were covered with metal or tough leather hides. Their spears were short or long, depending on the places in the battle where they were to fight. Short lances not more than two cubits long would be thrown at moving targets, and spears as long as six or seven cubits would be used to advance against the enemy in long lines of soldiers.

Archers were dressed much the same but with red belts and sashes and no helmets, so they could move more quickly. They used stout wooden bows and quivers full of arrows, which were slung over their shoulders.

On the wall, slingers and fighters with maces also wore metal helmets and carried metal shields in front of them.

As impressive as all this seemed, Caleb didn't feel safe. The day of judgment for Babylon had come, just as the prophet Daniel said it would. King Cyrus and his hordes of Medo-Persian warriors were finally here.

"I'm scared!" Caleb grabbed Tamzi's sleeve. "Guess I better go home and tell my family the news," he shouted as he headed for the stairs. With that, he was gone.

When he arrived at home, Mattaniah and several other gray-bearded elders from the Jewish synagogue were there, talking about the arrival of the Medo-Persian army. "Did you see the army approaching the city?" Mattaniah asked Caleb. "How many troops would you say they have?"

"It's hard to say yet." Caleb shrugged. "Thousands and thousands, I'd guess. The army stretches clear across the horizon."

"Then let us pray to the Lord our God," Mattaniah announced, and they knelt on the courtyard floor. "Oh Lord, our Lord, we call on You for help just now," he prayed.

> "The LORD executes righteousness
> And justice for all who are oppressed. . . .
> The LORD is merciful and gracious,
> Slow to anger, and abounding in mercy. . . .
> He has not dealt with us according to our sins,
> Nor punished us according to our iniquities.
> For as the heavens are high above the earth,
> So great is His mercy toward those who fear Him;
> As far as the east is from the west,
> So far has He removed our transgressions from us" (Psalm 103:6, 8, 10–12).

Caleb was in awe of the faith of these leaders. The Babylonians had been boasting for weeks that no one could conquer their city. No one could break through its fortifications, they had bragged, and now it seemed that everyone was in a panic.

But that was not the case with these elders. Their prayer for help was one of humble confidence. Mattaniah continued,

" 'As a father pities his children,
So the LORD pities those who fear Him.
For He knows our frame;
He remembers that we are dust. . . .
But the mercy of the LORD is from everlasting to everlasting
On those who fear Him,
And His righteousness to children's children,
To such as keep His covenant,
And to those who remember His commandments to do them. . . .
Bless the LORD, all His works,
In all places of His dominion.
Bless the LORD, O my soul!' " (verses 13, 14, 17, 18, 22).

The prayer was finished, and the elders remained on their knees. Caleb stayed on his knees, too, with his stomach tied in knots. This was the usual time of day to eat, but he could hardly think about that now. The elders had sent out a message to all the Jews that they should fast and pray, asking for God's protection in the days ahead. It made sense to Caleb. He should have been ravenous, but the only thing he could think about right now was King Cyrus and his hordes of Medo-Persian warriors.

"Help us, Lord God of our fathers," Caleb prayed, but his prayer seemed small and weak compared with the powerful army advancing on Babylon.

20

In every corner of Babylon, people were worried. The Medes and the Persians had finally arrived outside the city walls, and their frightening military machines were with them.

In the city, confidence was beginning to break down fast. Everywhere people were preparing for the worst. Men ran up the long flights of stairs to the guard towers to see what they could do to help. Mothers made their children stay near home. Merchants stockpiled food in their shops. Warlords directed soldiers as they stacked weapons and munitions in the guard towers along the wall.

Rumors from the palace didn't help either. In the royal court, the king's advisers were trying to get him to take the advancing Medo-Persian army seriously. "Cyrus is knocking on the door," they told King Belshazzar, "and he's serious!"

The king waved them off. "I'm serious too"—he laughed as he gulped more wine from his golden goblet—"serious about having a good time."

"He's not going away," they warned the king. "Cyrus has fought bigger armies than ours and whipped them all. He's faced greater challenges than Babylon and never flinched."

"Let him stay then, for all I care," Belshazzar slurred. "He can't starve us out, even if he waits forever. We've got enough food in the city to outlast him for twenty years."

Ishum, Belshazzar's minister of finance, leaned close to the king. "He'll find a way into the city, Your Majesty."

But Belshazzar paid little mind to the advisers' talk. He just laughed off their concerns, reminding them how safe everyone was behind the massive walls of Babylon.

The Jewish Day of Atonement was just a few days away. For the Jews, the Day of Atonement meant judgment for sins of the past, but it also meant freedom from evil in the future. With the arrival of the Medo-Persian army outside the city, every Jew was feeling the importance of that day even more. The Jews were captives in a foreign city, paying for the sins of their forefathers, but God in His mercy was about to show His hand of justice against their enemies.

That evening Jewish families gathered at the synagogue to pray again for God's forgiveness and protection. No one felt like singing, so they began a season of prayer. "Oh God, our help in ages past," Mattaniah prayed as he lifted his hands to heaven.

"In You, O Lord, I put my trust;
Let me never be ashamed;
Deliver me in Your righteousness.
Bow down Your ear to me,
Deliver me speedily;
Be my rock of refuge,
A fortress of defense to save me.
For You are my rock and my fortress;
Therefore, for Your name's sake,
Lead me and guide me."

The white-haired elder paused, then resumed as his voice filled with emotion.

"Pull me out of the net which [my enemies] have secretly laid for me,
For You are my strength.
Into Your hand I commit my spirit;
You have redeemed me, O Lord God of truth" (Psalm 31:1–5).

The prayer from Psalms encouraged everyone, but many were still worried—and not just about the Medo-Persian army waiting outside the walls of Babylon.

"It's the royal court we should be worried about most," Zaccai the scribe said as he stood to address the people. "King Belshazzar and his government officials are turning out to be our worst enemies." He lowered his voice. "He's not a smart ruler. He has failed to keep the surrounding nations under control as his grandfather did for so many decades. Now he's paying for it."

"That's the truth," Uncle Jabez replied. "Daniel himself said that judgments from Jehovah will come on Babylon because Belshazzar has been a wicked man. Rumors tell of wild, disgusting parties in the royal court for the king's friends and officials. He has chosen to glorify himself and the gods of Babylon, instead of Jehovah as Nebuchadnezzar finally did."

"I wish the prophet Daniel were here," Zaccai said sadly. "He would have words of wisdom for us."

Caleb whispered in his uncle's ear, "Why don't we see if he can come and talk with us now?"

Uncle Jabez glanced at Caleb and then stood to his feet. "Brother Zaccai, if you would like, I can go get Daniel."

Zaccai stared at Uncle Jabez for a moment. "You can reach him?"

"He gave me a pass should I need to get in touch with him," Uncle Jabez said. "I could have him here shortly, provided he's willing."

The scribe hesitated only a moment. "Go get him then. We'll sing and spend some more time in prayer until you return."

Uncle Jabez pulled Caleb to his feet. "We're on our way," he said, and out the door they went.

It wasn't far to Daniel's house. When they arrived at the gates of the government complex, Uncle Jabez showed the gatekeeper Daniel's pass. They found Daniel in good spirits. Though tired after a long day, he was willing to return with them to the synagogue.

"I'm glad to help any way I can," the prophet said with a smile. "Just give my servants a few minutes to harness the horses for my chariot, and we'll be on our way."

It was a tight fit as Caleb and his uncle squeezed in with Daniel and his two attendants, but the trip to the synagogue was a quick one.

When the three of them entered the synagogue, everyone began talking at once, but Daniel held up his hands for silence. "Peace be with you," he said in a commanding voice. "I am aware of the enemy that surrounds us on every side. However, I am here to tell you that God will not fail His people. He always keeps His promises. He is never late, and He never makes a mistake. My brothers and sisters, the seventy-year prophecy of Jeremiah will be fulfilled. It has to be. The promises of a coming Savior will not be fulfilled any other way."

Many in the congregation breathed a sigh of relief. "Praise God for His wonderful works to His people!" they said.

"This seventy-year prophecy," a young man named Kallai stood to his feet, "how do we know it isn't a conditional one?"

"Good question," Daniel nodded. "I'm here to tell you it is conditional on only one count. If we do not pray to our God and humbly confess our sins, we will not go home to Judah. It's plain and simple. Jehovah said it well when He challenged Solomon, our great king and ancestor with these words: 'If My people who are called by My name will humble themselves, and pray and seek My face, and turn from their wicked ways, then I will hear from heaven, and will forgive their sin and heal their land' " (2 Chronicles 7:14).

"But how will these things be?" Kallai persisted. "If Babylon is to be conquered and overrun by the Medes and the Persians, we can expect no mercy from them, especially the freedom to go back to Judah."

Daniel got a faraway look in his eyes. "It may seem hard for you to understand this prophecy now, but I'm here to say that it will be fulfilled. God's Word in the writings of Jeremiah will not return to Him empty, and He spells it out pretty clearly for us in that prophecy. However, there is a prophecy in the writings of Isaiah that interests me most."

Everyone sat up a little straighter at this comment, and the room began to buzz. Daniel held up his hand for silence. "My dear brothers and sisters," he said, "the hour is late, and we are tired from an exhausting day. I came here tonight to encourage you, but there is so much more to say. If you will come again tomorrow night, I will show you the prophecy of which I speak in the writings of Isaiah."

He surveyed the small congregation gathered in the synagogue. "And now peace be to you!" he said as he disappeared into the night.

21

It had been a solemn prayer meeting, and the truth was beginning to set in. The prophecy of Jeremiah was there for all to see, but no one was sure how it would be fulfilled now with the arrival of the armies of King Cyrus. Would the Medes and the Persians have anything to do with the final outcome of that prophecy?

Then there was the prophecy of Isaiah, the one Daniel had talked about just before he left the synagogue. *It must be important, or Daniel wouldn't have mentioned it*, Caleb thought.

The meeting broke up as the people left for home, but there was concern on every face.

Caleb and Uncle Jabez stayed to talk with the scribe. "Do you know anything about that prophecy in the writings of Isaiah?" Uncle Jabez asked. "The one Daniel spoke of?"

"I'm not sure which one he meant, but we'll find out soon enough," Zaccai said. He went to the Scripture cabinet and pulled out one of the sacred scrolls with the writings of Isaiah. "Let me do some studying myself before we meet again tomorrow night."

Uncle Jabez stared at the scroll in Zaccai's hands. "Do you think it's good news or bad?"

"I'm hoping it's good news." Zaccai tapped the scroll with his fingers and then frowned ominously. "One thing's for certain: things are probably going to get worse now before they get better."

On the way home, Caleb was quieter than usual, and Uncle Jabez noticed it. "Everybody's worried, and with good reason," he said as he laid a hand on Caleb's shoulder. "But we don't need to be. God is our Protector."

"Yeah, I know." Caleb stared up at the night sky. "But I'm just wondering. We've all been talking about Jeremiah's seventy-year prophecy. How are we going to be set free to go back to Judah if the Medes and the Persians conquer Babylon?"

Uncle Jabez nodded. "Good question, Caleb. I can't say I know the answer to that. However, I've heard King Cyrus is a good ruler and that he is fair to the Medes and the Persians."

"Yeah, but will he be good to the Babylonians and Jews, too, if he conquers this city?"

"That remains to be seen." Uncle Jabez breathed in the evening air deeply. "We can always hope."

Caleb had a hard time falling asleep again that night. He tossed and turned while thinking about the seventy-year prophecy and the Medo-Persian army camped outside the walls of Babylon. He thought about Belshazzar and his wild parties in the palace, and then again there was the mystery of the temple treasures sitting in the warehouse. Finally, he fell asleep, but his dreams were a jumbled mess of enemy soldiers, loud party music, and mysterious treasures hidden away in wooden crates.

The next morning Caleb awoke with a start. He immediately remembered the events from the night before and jumped up from his sleeping mat. He rushed through his chores and gulped down some breakfast. The holiday feasts were coming up, and during that time, he wouldn't have to go to school. The Day of Atonement was a serious time of year, and the Feast of Tabernacles that followed was the most exciting holiday of all for a boy.

Life had changed for everyone in the city of Babylon. People were so worried about the enemy soldiers outside the walls that they didn't even go to the markets to do business. No one sat in the narrow streets selling fruits or vegetables. No one hung their meats up in the meat market. No one was buying carpets or jewelry or clothing. That meant there was no point in taking the finished pottery to the marketplace as Caleb usually did.

Instead people gathered in small groups to talk on street corners and at the local city wells. Would the Medes and the Persians try to starve them out? Would they launch thousands of flaming arrows at the Babylonian soldiers on the walls? Would the enemy find a weakness in the formidable fortifications of Babylon?

Caleb went up on the wall with Tamzi several times that day to help prepare for the inevitable battle. More enemy soldiers would come. More war engines would be brought down the road from Sippar. Cyrus the Great would eventually show up at the head of the Medo-Persian military machine, and that brought Babylonian generals together to figure out what to do next.

Many who came to see the spectacle from the top of the stout Babylonian walls were terrified. "We're doomed!" they wailed. "When the Medes and the Persians finally break through these walls, they'll carve us up and feed us to the jackals and vultures."

But others just laughed scornfully. "We're not afraid of you Persian dogs," they shouted, shaking their fists at the lines of enemy soldiers stretching in a band around the city. "Why don't you Medes climb up these walls and fight like men? Even the blind and lame of Babylon could keep you out of this city!"

Guards in the watchtowers seemed divided on the seriousness of the situation too. Some seemed unaffected by the sight of enemy soldiers and war machines encircling the city. Others made frequent trips to the shrines of their pagan gods when they weren't at their posts of duty on the city wall. Offerings of meat and money to Ishtar and Marduk, however, didn't give them much peace.

More news of the palace drifted onto the streets. King Belshazzar was still having one drunken party after another. Some were saying celebrations like that would lift the spirits of those in the city, but many like Caleb were just as sure the king couldn't bring himself to face the truth.

"He's too arrogant to know better," Caleb told Tamzi. "His nonstop parties show he's nothing but a coward and unwilling to face his doom. It's the only way he can hide his fear of the Medes and the Persians."

By late that afternoon, more Medo-Persian soldiers arrived from Sippar and Opis. Thousands upon thousands of them came, until they seemed to surround the expansive city of Babylon. A battery of catapults and spear-throwers followed, along with an army of donkeys and oxen to transport them. Caleb noticed there were no battering rams. He was sure the Medes and Persians understood such war engines would never work on a city such as Babylon.

There was a wide, deep moat surrounding Babylon, and if that didn't stop invaders, the walls would. Sand and debris had been dumped between the high double walls that stretched around the city. Such fortifications would never break down under the incessant pounding of a battering ram.

It had been a long day. Everything seemed turned upside down to Caleb. Fear was written on every face in the streets of Babylon, and everyone everywhere seemed in a panic.

Caleb was worried too. By sunset, he realized he hadn't thought about the seventy-year prophecy that whole day, and he hadn't once thought about the temple relics from Judah either.

At the evening meal, Uncle Jabez told everyone he had heard the king was planning a weeklong feast for a thousand of his most powerful lords. Government officers, army generals, rich merchants, and their wives would be wined and dined like never before.

What's next? Caleb wondered. *Doesn't King Belshazzar have any common sense? Doesn't he have any fear of the doom hanging over his kingdom? Evidently not.*

22

Suddenly Caleb remembered the meeting Daniel had promised them. The prophet would be coming to the synagogue in just a few minutes to talk with everyone about a mysterious prophecy in the writings of Isaiah.

Caleb ate his lentil stew faster than usual and stuffed two pieces of flatbread under the belt of his tunic to eat on the way. "Come on!" he jumped up from the family circle. "We've got to hurry if we want to get good seats in the synagogue. We're going to be late!"

They hurried off to the synagogue together. On the way, they met Tamzi going in the opposite direction. "You want to come to the synagogue with us to hear some breaking news?" Caleb said.

"What's it all about?" Tamzi asked.

Caleb shrugged. "We know as much as you. It's something about a strange prophecy."

"I'm in," Tamzi replied, and the two boys rushed on to the synagogue, leaving Caleb's family behind.

Daniel hadn't yet arrived when the boys reached the synagogue. They watched the road for him, however, and when they finally spotted his chariot, they ran to meet him.

The waiting Jewish worshipers welcomed Daniel warmly and then invited him to pray for them. "Oh, God, our help in ages past," Daniel said, "we ask You tonight to forgive our sins and to restore us to Your favor. Dangers are all around, and You alone can rescue us. Hear our prayer, oh Lord."

Caleb felt the presence of God in that meeting, and it was a good feeling. He knew he should be scared of the plans the Medo-Persian army might have for Babylon; but right now, his mind was at peace.

"Thank you for inviting me here," Daniel said as he held up a scroll he had brought with him. "I promised I would return tonight to share a prophecy with you from the writings of the prophet Isaiah. They were written about one hundred and fifty years ago, but that makes no difference when we're talking about the prophecies of Jehovah. We know there's no one like Him, who declares ' "the end from the beginning, and from ancient times things not yet done" ' " (Isaiah 46:10).

As he opened the scroll he had brought with him, Daniel said, "This is what I found:

" 'Thus says the LORD to His anointed,
To Cyrus, whose right hand I have held—
To subdue nations before him
And loose the armor of kings,
To open before him the double doors,
So that the gates will not be shut:
"I will go before you
And make the crooked places straight;
I will break in pieces the gates of bronze
And cut the bars of iron.
I will give you the treasures of darkness
And hidden riches of secret places,
That you may know that I, the LORD,
Who call you by your name,
Am the God of Israel" ' " (Isaiah 45:1–3).

No one in the congregation moved, and every eye was on the old prophet.

"You're probably wondering who this Cyrus is," Daniel added. "Well, the previous passage makes this prophecy even more interesting. Isaiah writes of Cyrus,

> " ' "He is My shepherd,
> And he shall perform all My pleasure,
> Saying to Jerusalem, 'You shall be built,'
> And to the temple, 'Your foundation shall be laid' " ' " (Isaiah 44:28).

Daniel let his words sink in. Silence filled the room, and Caleb glanced around at everyone, wondering if the prophet's words had hit their mark.

Caleb finally raised his hand, hesitant to ask the question he knew must be on everyone's mind. "Is the Persian king the Cyrus Isaiah is talking about?" he asked.

"Good question." Daniel winked at Caleb. "This passage says a ruler named Cyrus will set God's people free and help them rebuild their temple. That's quite a prophecy! So, as you asked, is this King Cyrus of Persia indeed the one Isaiah was talking about? If you're like me, you're probably wondering how's that going to happen." The prophet shook his head and started to roll up the scroll. "We can't say for certain, but there's no doubt God has a thousand ways to fulfill His Word. He can do it through Belshazzar, Cyrus, or any other ruler He wants.

"Now don't forget, the day after tomorrow is our great Day of Atonement ceremony," Daniel said as he prepared to leave the synagogue. "We've been so busy and so worried lately about the arrival of the Medo-Persian army. But God has a special blessing for us on that day, even if we are far from our ancestral home, and even if our glorious temple is no more. On the Day of Atonement, the Lord God of our fathers has promised to cleanse us of every sin."

No one said much of anything on the way home that night. Not even Grandpa Obed. They were too busy thinking about the prophecy that Daniel had read to them from the writings of Isaiah.

But Caleb's mind was going nonstop. *If Cyrus and the Medes and the Persians are to overthrow Babylon, how will they do it? Will they try to starve the people of Babylon into submission? Will they find a way to break through the walls of the city, or do they have some other trick up their sleeve?*

The next morning military officers went through neighborhoods across Babylon, asking for more volunteers to help the city prepare for battle. Caleb and Tamzi went along to work with Isi. They hauled giant stones in wagons up long ramps to the top of the city wall. The stones weighed as much as two talents each and would be used in the giant catapults near the guard towers.

While they worked, Isi shared some late-breaking news with the boys. "There's something really strange going on in the Medo-Persian army," he said. "For two nights now, they have camped along the western and northern walls of Babylon, but this is the second day they have disappeared in the west around the bend in the Euphrates River. No one really knew what they were doing until military scouts came back with news that the army was digging a canal."

"A canal? For what?" Caleb grunted as he helped Tamzi roll another large stone up a plank on to the wagon.

"Who knows? My guess is they need extra water for something. Their horses, maybe? Some military machine?"

That afternoon a royal crier came running through the streets with important news. Caleb and Tamzi leaned over the inside wall to listen as the runner stopped to make his announcement at the Ishtar Gate.

"Tomorrow at this time a procession of government officials will pass through the main boulevard on a parade to the palace," he called out in an official monotone. "They will be joining King Belshazzar and the royal family for a feast to end all feasts! Please clear the street at that time."

Caleb went home that evening after hauling catapult stones the entire day. From dawn until dusk he had worked, but his day wasn't done. Aunt Helah sent him to the market to bring home the last of the clay pots and jars from their market stall. "Better to be safe than sorry," she said. "We could be in for some rough days ahead with rioting and looting in the streets."

Grandpa Obed was ill, and Uncle Jabez was at the synagogue, getting ready for the solemn Day of Atonement celebration. That meant Caleb had to work alone. It took him longer than usual, but he managed to get all the pots and jars loaded into the donkey cart by dark.

Uncle Jabez didn't come home for the evening meal, so the family sat down without him. The meal was a simple one of figs and flatbread in preparation for the holy day to come on the morrow.

"Don't forget to take a bath before you go to bed," Aunt Helah reminded Caleb. "Also, I've laid out your special tunic for the ceremony in the morning."

Caleb knew he should be looking forward to the solemn day, but he had to admit that he wasn't. On that day, no one was allowed to eat. Everyone fasted, and that made it hard for him to get through the day.

"Lord, please help me get in the spirit of the day," he prayed as he went to sleep that night. "Tomorrow all our sins will be washed away for good. It's the day when You make our nation as white as snow."

23

The next morning dawned bright and clear and promised to be a cool one for a change. Caleb hurried through his chores and then got into his best clothes. By the third hour, he was ready to go with his family to the synagogue.

Most of the important families in Caleb's Jewish community were at the synagogue to worship. All of Caleb's cousins were there, and most of the boys from his school. Jemi was there, too, sitting with the girls and women. Once he caught her looking at him, and it made him feel good inside. He had never felt this way about anyone before.

As Caleb listened while Zaccai read from the Scriptures, he tried to concentrate, but it was hard. How could he focus on what Zaccai was saying when he remembered that thousands of enemy soldiers were getting ready to attack right outside the wall?

Besides that, his stomach was growling. It was the Day of Atonement, and everyone was fasting.

Quoting a psalm, Zaccai prayed with his hands lifted to heaven as he stood before the congregation:

"Have mercy upon me, O God,
According to Your lovingkindness;
According to the multitude of Your tender mercies,
Blot out my transgressions.
Wash me thoroughly from my iniquity,
And cleanse me from my sin.
For I acknowledge my transgressions,
And my sin is always before me.
Against You, You only, have I sinned,
And done this evil in Your sight—
That You may be found just when You speak,
And blameless when You judge" (Psalm 51:1–4).

"This should be our prayer every day," Zaccai said solemnly, "but it is especially important on this holy Day of Atonement. King David said it well,

"Purge me with hyssop, and I shall be clean;
Wash me, and I shall be whiter than snow.
Make me hear joy and gladness,
That the bones You have broken may rejoice.
Hide Your face from my sins,
And blot out all my iniquities.
Create in me a clean heart, O God,
And renew a steadfast spirit within me.
Do not cast me away from Your presence,
And do not take Your Holy Spirit from me.
Restore to me the joy of Your salvation,
And uphold me by Your generous Spirit" (verses 7–12).

Zaccai talked about how the Day of Atonement had gotten its start in the ancient kingdom of Israel. He told how the high priest chose two goats. One was sacrificed, and its blood was sprinkled before the ark of the covenant. The other goat was called a scapegoat. The high priest put his hands on the scapegoat and transferred all the sins from Israel to the goat. Then the goat was sent out to die in the wilderness.

It was a very special day, indeed! Caleb had always revered the Day of Atonement, but this year he realized it was even more important and should mean even more to him. Maybe the nearness of the enemy outside the walls of Babylon was part of it. Maybe the coming troubles helped him to understand just how much he needed a Savior and how happy he was to have his sins forgiven.

At noon, as the family was walking home, they heard musical instruments playing and the shout of a public crier. "It must be the procession they said would come!" Caleb shouted excitedly. "Can I go up on the wall and watch?"

"It's the Day of Atonement," Uncle Jabez glanced at Aunt Helah and then turned to Caleb. "You may go for a few minutes," he said, laying a hand on Caleb's shoulder, "but then hurry home. This is a holy day to the Lord."

The procession was a grand one, and it lasted all afternoon. Caleb didn't have time to see it all; but if he had, he would have seen a thousand visitors on their way to the palace where a grand banquet was planned. Governors, magistrates, generals, and statesmen came dressed in the best of robes, with elaborate chains of gold around their necks. They came in carriages and chariots, on majestic steeds and mules. What a parade this turned out to be! The most influential people in the city showed up, and with them came their entourages of wives and personal attendants.

At home, the family gathered in the courtyard to sing and pray and read their favorite passages of Scripture. Grandpa Obed and Uncle Jabez told stories about God's people from the past, and by early evening, other family members began to show up for the occasion. Several aunts and uncles and cousins came, and Jemi was there too.

Tamzi came over to take part, even though there was no food. "I don't know how you do it," he told Caleb. "I can't stand to go more than a few hours without eating. You've gone all day! Since last night, right?"

"Don't remind me," Caleb rolled his eyes and then felt guilty for saying it. "But really, Tamzi, it's not so bad," he laughed. "I shouldn't complain. There are reasons we fast like this. It's to remind us how blessed we are to have plenty of food. It's a time for us to remember we're God's people."

"Oh, and, of course, there's the part about our sins," he added. "We fast to give us time to ask forgiveness for our sins. That's the most important reason of all. God forgives us of all the bad things we do, but He wants us to remember there's a price for sin."

"Really. That's how it works?" Tamzi was listening to every word Caleb was saying. "And what's the price for sin?"

"Death."

"Death? *Hmm.*" Tamzi got a strange look in his eye. "But you don't sacrifice people like other religions do. The gods Babylonians worship sometimes demand that, but your God doesn't. Why is that?"

There was so much going on in the family courtyard, with everyone laughing and talking and having a good time; but Caleb realized what was happening. God was giving him a chance to explain some things to his best friend about how the Jews worshiped.

"We all should have to die," Caleb continued. "We're all sinners, but God wants us to have eternal life. He doesn't want us to die. That's why the promised Messiah will come someday to die for us, and when He does, the price for sin will be paid by the Lamb of God."

"And?" Tamzi kept staring at Caleb.

Caleb could see his friend was confused. "Let me start over," he said. "In the very beginning, the first man and woman on earth lived in paradise. It was a garden home the Creator Jehovah had made for them. It was a beautiful place with no fighting or sickness or death. Everything was perfect, but that all ended when the evil prince of darkness convinced the man and woman to turn against Jehovah. They believed his lies and lost their home in paradise."

"Really?" Tamzi squinted at Caleb. "And who was the evil prince of darkness?"

"The evil prince is a dark angel who fell from heaven because he rebelled against Jehovah."

"He still exists?" Tamzi's eyes grew wide with surprise.

"He does."

"And that first man and woman were stupid enough to listen to him instead of Jehovah?"

"You got it." Caleb smiled at Tamzi, glad to see that Tamzi was catching on to the unusual stories of salvation that most kids would never understand. "It seems hard to believe when we look back at it now." Caleb shrugged. "But that's what happened. Jehovah was very sad at how things had turned out for the man and woman. He had created paradise for the man and woman, but now they would have to pay for their sin."

Tamzi frowned. "How would they do that?"

Caleb sighed. "That was the sad part. Jehovah said they would have to die."

"Oh, like an execution or something?"

"Yeah, kind of; but it was different. They had to leave the garden. You know, that's where God had planted the tree of life for them. Eating the fruit would have kept them alive forever; but without the tree of life, they would die."

"Wow! That's an awful story." Tamzi shook his head. "I've heard it before but never quite like that."

"Yeah, well, it doesn't end there," Caleb added confidently. "Jehovah told the man and woman He had a plan. One day He would send the Lamb of God to die for them, so they could come back to their garden home."

Tamzi stared at Caleb again. "Really? So who is this Lamb of God? Is it a real lamb?"

"No, not a real lamb. That's just a symbol, and it's why we sacrifice lambs when we worship. It represents the One who will die for us."

"So who is it?" Tamzi asked again. "Who will be the Messiah you're talking about?"

"Jehovah," Caleb replied. "It will be Jehovah Himself." He was surprised that Tamzi was so interested in such things. Tamzi was a Babylonian, and most people from Babylon thought of the Jews as inferior. After all, Jews were captives, prisoners of war from a distant land.

24

Jehovah! What do you mean Jehovah?" Tamzi almost shouted. "Not the Jehovah you say is your God!"

"That's Him." Caleb didn't blink. He was so focused on their conversation that he never noticed Saarah and Jemi come up behind them to see what they were talking about.

"That's crazy! I don't get it," Tamzi kept saying. "I never heard of such a thing in all my life. Why would your God, Jehovah, come and be a sacrifice for you? Gods don't die for humans. Tammuz wouldn't do that, and neither would Ishtar! And Marduk? Ha!" Tamzi almost laughed. "Especially not Marduk."

Caleb realized how strange this all must sound to Tamzi. He was trying hard to explain it to his best friend in a way that didn't sound hokey, but it wasn't easy. Right now Tamzi was probably having a hard time believing anything Caleb was telling him.

But not Jemi. She and Saarah had been listening all along to the things Caleb was saying. "I get it," Jemi said matter-of-factly. "It kind of makes sense to me."

Caleb and Tamzi turned suddenly to see Jemi standing there with Saarah.

"It's the most romantic thing I ever heard, and I like it," Jemi said softly. She had such a look of faith and sweetness that Caleb didn't know what to say.

"Really?" was all he could manage.

"Where do you get this stuff?" Tamzi asked suddenly. His eyes turned beady with suspicion.

"From our Scriptures." Caleb looked at Tamzi in surprise. *What is happening to Tamzi? Is the evil one coming into our conversation to steal Tamzi's heart away? This is no time for Tamzi to doubt the Word of God. Not with all he has learned about the prophecies that are soon to be fulfilled. Not with the armies of the Medes and the Persians just outside the walls of Babylon!* Caleb sent a prayer to heaven, asking Jehovah to give him the right words to say.

"It's in our Scriptures," he repeated with conviction. "The patriarchs and prophets wrote down the words of God from long ago, so we would have a record of it."

"You mean those scrolls you read from in your synagogue?"

"That's them."

"It's all in there?" Tamzi looked like he was calming down again.

"Yup! We can read more about it if you want sometime."

"I'd like that." Tamzi's eyes softened, and Caleb breathed a sigh of relief. It was clear God had intervened and sent the evil one away. Caleb lifted his eyes to heaven, glad to have given Tamzi something to think about.

Caleb noticed Jemi staring at him again. The only thing he could think to say was, "What?"

"Oh, nothing, I was just thinking of how different you and Saarah are," she said with a look of admiration. "My family hardly knows anything about the Scriptures. We're Jews, but everyone in my family is only interested in their businesses. We're weavers, and my family makes a lot of money doing that; but I wish we would read more from the scrolls like your family does. You know so much about Jehovah," she continued, "and Saarah is always memorizing verses from the scrolls you have at your house. Where did you get those scrolls, anyway?"

"We copied them. Mostly my uncle and grandpa did, but I got to help some too."

"Really?" Jemi seemed even more impressed.

Caleb shrugged. "Yeah, lots of families have done that here in Babylon. We don't have very many copies; so if we want to read the Scriptures at home, we make copies. But we have to be very careful," he added. "We can't make mistakes when we spell the words because it's the Word of God, you know."

"I'm sure you're right." With a look of innocence, Jemi said, "It all sounds so mysterious. You have to be very serious about this stuff if you're going to be copying all those prophecies in the scrolls. I've been hearing lots about them lately. The prophecies of Jeremiah and Isaiah, I mean. We don't go to the synagogue all the time, but even my folks are talking about it now," Jemi added. "I suppose you know lots about the prophecies too?"

"Some." Caleb didn't want to brag, but the prophecies were now all that he thought about. In fact, they had become the most important things in his life—that and the secret of the sacred treasures hidden in the royal warehouse.

Jemi kept staring at Caleb, and it made him want to blush.

When Saarah leaned toward Caleb and whispered, "She likes you," Caleb squirmed. "Come on." He grabbed Tamzi's sleeve, while his face turned an even brighter shade. "Let's go up on the roof to watch the stars." Off they went, leaving the girls to giggle on their own.

The long day finally ended, but even as Caleb lay on his mat that night he could hear the distant drone of music coming from the palace on the evening wind. The party King Belshazzar was holding for his government friends was getting out of hand. They would dance and drink into the wee hours of the morning, oblivious to the dangers of the Medo-Persian army just outside Babylon's walls. They would do all kinds of evil things as they worshiped their foolish idols of gold and stone. They would ignore the ominous warnings of the king's closest advisers that doom was at the door.

Despite all that, there was a warm spot in Caleb's chest. He couldn't get Jemi, with her pretty face and sweet ways, out of his mind. She was interested in the Scriptures. That part was really important to him. Other than that, he didn't know much about her. *Does she understand that the days of Jeremiah's seventy-year prophecy are almost up? Does she know that Isaiah mentioned King Cyrus by name as the one who will write a decree to set the Jews free?*

He didn't know if Jemi knew about any of these things. If she came to the synagogue more, she soon would. That's all that people were talking about these days.

The next morning the news from the sentries on the wall was the same. The strange activities of the Medo-Persian army continued. The enemy soldiers were not in camp, and it was assumed they were working on the canal. But why they wanted a canal was still a mystery. There was plenty of fresh water in the river for the Medo-Persian army.

The guards were now doubled at every watchtower, and the iron gates of the city were being reinforced—triple thick. Babylon was on full alert.

Caleb's classes were not being held because the city was in a state of emergency. Uncle Jabez and Grandpa Obed puttered around in the shop, though, making a few small clay pots and jars, and Caleb helped them. It was better to keep his mind busy.

That morning Tamzi came over and helped Caleb in the pottery shop. As they worked together treading clay in the kneading trough, they talked about the latest news on the street. They talked about the things Daniel had shared with the congregation at the synagogue, and they continued the conversation they had been having about Jehovah, the God of heaven.

"Tell me more about your God," Tamzi said. "You and your family are different. The people at your synagogue are not like everyone else I know. Is that because of your religion? Is that because you're Jews?"

Caleb thought for a moment. "Yeah, it's true. Our religion does make us different, but that's because of the God we worship. Jehovah is His name, the Creator of heaven and earth. He's the One who will someday come to this world Himself to rescue His people from war and pain and death. In the meantime, He asks us to be fair and kind. He wants us to walk humbly with Him."

"Is that why Daniel is such a good man? Because he worships your God, Jehovah?" Tamzi squinted at Caleb. "The dreams and visions he talks about sound like they actually come from the gods."

Caleb smiled. "Yeah, well, that's because they do. He gets his messages from Jehovah. Remember the dream he had years ago that was the same one King Nebuchadnezzar had? The one about the image he asked Jehovah to give him? If that's not proof enough about the power of my God, I don't know what is."

"Can't argue with you there." Tamzi stopped treading the clay. "It seems your God is more powerful than any god we've ever worshiped here in Babylon. The more I hear about Him, the more I believe He's the one true God."

During the midday meal, a messenger from Tamzi's house showed up. He bowed respectfully to Uncle Jabez and Grandpa Obed as he entered the family courtyard. "Master Malik kindly asks that you come to the archive warehouse immediately. He says it's an emergency."

Uncle Jabez glanced at Caleb as if reading his mind. "We'd be glad to help," he said.

Caleb quickly drank the stew from his bowl, grabbed some extra bread, and jumped up. "Come on; let's go now," he said.

25

Caleb and Uncle Jabez rushed out the door. When they got to the warehouse, they got the shock of their lives.

"I had visitors this morning!" Malik exclaimed. "Balasu, the royal steward, came in, looking for the best golden goblets and cups in the warehouse. The minute I saw him, I knew he was up to no good."

Malik took Caleb and Uncle Jabez into the warehouse chamber where the crates from Judah were stored. "I've got a bad feeling about this," he admitted as they all stared at the crates still lying on the floor. Caleb could see that many more crates had been opened, and some of the lids were off the crates, exposing the precious artifacts inside.

"When Balasu saw your holy relics from ancient Judah, he seemed very happy," Malik added. "He examined many of the golden artifacts in these crates and had his scribe make notations about them on his ledger. I'm sorry to say it, but I'm afraid he's going to use them at the king's banquet in the palace."

Caleb's mouth dropped open in horror at the terrible news. He wanted to scream. *No, not this! Not the sacred vessels from God's temple in Jerusalem! The temple is gone, of course—destroyed by Nebuchadnezzar's invading army—but God has been good to allow some of the artifacts of gold and silver to survive. They were safe and sound in this warehouse, having survived almost seventy years away from their homeland. And now this! The royal steward wants to take them away to be used in a wicked party of dancing and drinking and who knows what else! It is unthinkable!*

"Did he take any of the temple vessels with him?" Uncle Jabez asked.

"No, not yet, but I'm guessing he will. He said he'd be back soon." Malik had a pained look on his face. "It's just a matter of time," he said sadly.

Caleb felt the bottom of his world dropping away. "This is a disaster!" He grabbed his uncle's arm. "We just found the holy vessels. God won't let the steward take them away now, will He?"

Uncle Jabez's face looked white. "It is bad news," he admitted, "but you have to remember we're captives in Babylon and so are the holy vessels. That takes this completely out of our hands." Caleb had never seen him so upset. "However, we should also realize that God can take care of the cups and goblets no matter where they are. He's been watching them here in Babylon for almost seventy years, and He's guarding them now."

That evening Caleb and his family went to the synagogue to welcome the Sabbath. Only a few people were there, but Tamzi came and, wonder of wonders, Malik showed up too.

Evidently Tamzi had been talking with his father about the things he had been learning from Caleb. No doubt he had been sharing the prophecies that said Babylon would fall and the Jews would be allowed to go home.

For Malik, the most amazing thing of all was the fact that the prophecies had been made decades before. And now it looked like they might actually have a chance to be fulfilled.

Zaccai led the congregation as they sang some Hebrew songs, and then he quoted a passage from a scroll of the Psalms. "He who dwells in the secret place of the Most High shall abide under the shadow of the Almighty," he recited, and the congregation joined in. Even Caleb knew the psalm by heart.

> "I will say of the Lord, 'He is my refuge and my fortress;
> My God, in Him I will trust.'
> Surely He shall deliver you from the snare of the fowler
> And from the perilous pestilence.

He shall cover you with His feathers,
And under His wings you shall take refuge;
His truth shall be your shield and buckler.
You shall not be afraid of the terror by night,
Nor of the arrow that flies by day,
Nor of the pestilence that walks in darkness,
Nor of the destruction that lays waste at noonday" (Psalm 91:1–6).

Caleb could feel the power in the psalm of deliverance. It was like God Himself was in the room with them, and Caleb was sure He was. There was no way to explain the feeling of peace that had come over him.

"A thousand may fall at your side,
And ten thousand at your right hand;
But it shall not come near you.
Only with your eyes shall you look,
And see the reward of the wicked.
Because you have made the LORD, who is my refuge,
Even the Most High, your dwelling place,
No evil shall befall you,
Nor shall any plague come near your dwelling;
For He shall give His angels charge over you,
To keep you in all your ways" (verses 7–11).

The next morning Caleb's family showed up at the synagogue for the Sabbath worship service, but again many of the Jews were not in attendance. Their faith was evidently being tested by the threat of the Medo-Persian siege.

But Malik and Tamzi were there. They were Babylonians, and yet their hearts had been stirred by what they had heard the night before. Caleb felt as if his heart would jump right out of his chest. He was so glad to see them worshiping Jehovah in the synagogue! Clearly, the Spirit of God was speaking to their hearts.

Daniel was there, too, and his message of encouragement was also a warning. "Babylon will soon fall," he said solemnly. "Prophecy foretells it in the writings of Isaiah, Jeremiah, and Ezekiel. It's just a matter of time now."

Daniel shook his head sadly, "King Belshazzar is too arrogant to care and too stubborn to change. His advisers in the palace are telling him the kingdom is about to collapse. His foreign ambassadors have been warning him for several years that he needs to secure the borders of the Babylonian Empire, but he won't listen. What he needs to do is spend less time throwing parties in Babylon and more time defending the outposts of his kingdom.

The latest rumor is that the Medes and the Persians may have found a weakness in Babylon's fortifications," Daniel added. "Cyrus is a brilliant general, and many of Babylon's military advisers are sure he's already found one."

Silence gripped the group of worshipers in the synagogue. No one spoke aloud, and it seemed hardly a soul breathed.

Uncle Jabez finally broke the silence. "Where's the weakness?" he asked.

"We don't really know." Daniel shook his head. "But many believe it may have something to do with the gates of Babylon."

"Then we had better call on the Lord our God," Uncle Jabez said. "If they can breach the gates, we're finished."

"You're right," Daniel said. "What we need to do now is pray. Pray as we have never prayed before, and stay close to our homes. If the Medo-Persian army invades the city, they will surely slaughter anyone running in the streets."

That evening Caleb went to the west wall to get a look at the enemy camp sprawled across the plain. The sunset cast its glowing colors across the landscape, turning everything a rosy red and then lavender. The smoke of a thousand campfires had settled in the river valley like a blanket of fog. The enemy soldiers were returning to their campsites in long lines from the west. It was still a mystery why they were going upriver every day to dig that canal and then came back in the evenings all tired and worn out.

When darkness had come, Caleb went back home and to bed, but he couldn't sleep. He kept remembering Daniel's words of judgment about the approaching destruction, but that wasn't what kept him awake longer than usual. He could hear music from the palace floating on the evening air.

Finally, he fell asleep sometime in the night. Not surprisingly he dreamed, but his dreams were nightmares. Strange shadows of enemy soldiers storming the walls of Babylon ran through his head. Weapons clashed, flaming arrows flew up over the walls, and screams of the wounded, dying Babylonians filled the air.

Suddenly, his dreams were interrupted by shouting and loud pounding on the courtyard gate. Caleb awoke with a start and was strangely disoriented by the commotion. *Who is at the gate this time of night?* he wondered as he tried to clear the fog from his mind.

"Open the gate," a voice kept shouting, "Open up, I say! There's trouble at the palace!" Suddenly, Caleb was on his feet. He raced down the stairs to the gate, his uncle Jabez right behind him.

It was Tamzi, who was holding a torch in his hand and had one of his father's servants with him. "He did it!" Tamzi was shouting. "The palace steward came to the warehouse and took Jehovah's sacred vessels!"

26

They're gone?" Caleb stammered. "All of them?"

"Yup! He came to get them an hour ago. My father tried to stop him. He told him anyone who uses the sacred vessels for unholy purposes would be cursed! They belong to Jehovah, the God of heaven, my father told him, but Balasu just laughed. He brought wagons with him and a squadron of soldiers and loaded up the crates of golden cups and goblets anyway."

Caleb's mind was whirling. Everything was crazy and spinning out of control just as Daniel had predicted. It was like one of the nightmares he had been having before he awoke, and he wanted to shake himself to make the bad news go away.

But it wasn't a dream. It was as real as the flaming torch in Tamzi's hand.

"Come on!" Tamzi shouted again. "We've got to get word to Daniel! The sacred vessels are already on their way to the palace."

"Where's your father now?"

"He's going to meet us at Daniel's house."

Caleb put on an outer tunic and ran to get his sandals. *The world is coming apart, for certain! Everything is going wrong. Enemy soldiers are threatening to take Babylon. King Belshazzar and his lords are drinking up a storm, while ignoring the threat of invasion by the Medes and the Persians. And now the ancient vessels from Jehovah's temple have been taken away to be used at a wild party!*

Caleb and Tamzi raced away with Uncle Jabez into the darkness. The moon was now rising up over the eastern wall of the city. Within minutes, they arrived out of breath at the gates to the palace grounds. Amazingly, the gates were wide open. Caleb could hear giddy music coming from the palace's banquet hall, but the guards were nowhere in sight.

"Wait a minute," Uncle Jabez held up his hand, as though afraid to take Caleb and Tamzi through the open gateway. "We can't go in there without permission."

"But you have the pass Daniel gave us," Caleb protested. "That should get us in."

Uncle Jabez glanced through the gateway and up the promenade toward the palace complex. "What about the guards?" he said. "Where are they? I don't want them to think we're intruders."

Unexpectedly, Caleb heard something behind the wall at one side of the gate. It sounded like snoring; when he stuck his head around the corner, he almost laughed. Two guards were there. One was sitting on the ground, leaning against the wall, and the other was lying with his face to the pavement.

"I can't believe these guys are sleeping," Tamzi said. "Guards aren't supposed to sleep on duty."

"They're probably drunk." Caleb went behind the wall to get a closer look.

Tamzi picked up a clay cup lying on the ground and took a whiff. "Yup, they've been drinking." He handed the cup to Uncle Jabez.

Uncle Jabez glanced toward the palace. "Someone must have brought them the wine," he said. "With the party going on inside, everybody's probably drinking. From the sounds of that music, it's like the biggest holiday of the year."

"Come on. We've got to get going," Caleb announced. "We're supposed to go warn Daniel about the sacred vessels, and Tamzi's father will be waiting for us too."

Uncle Jabez hesitated but only for a moment. "OK, everybody is either sleeping or drunk. Let's go."

They hurried up the promenade and then down the dimly lit pathways, passing gardens and courtyards full of people having parties. The music was loud, and the food smelled delicious, but Caleb had no time to think about either.

Within minutes, they were standing at the gate to Daniel's apartment suite. Malik was there ahead of them, already telling Daniel about the holy vessels the palace steward had taken.

The old prophet laid a hand on the boys' shoulders to assure them. "There's nothing more we could have done. It's all in God's hands now," he said quietly. "It's a sad day for the Jews and will most certainly be a terrible day of judgment for Babylon."

Caleb knew Daniel was right. It was over. The evil one had inspired bad people to take the holy vessels of God. They would most surely defile them with their wine and food.

Does God even care? Caleb wondered. For a moment, he was tempted to think the Lord had abandoned His people. *If Jehovah can't keep the temple treasures safe, why would He do anything for His people? The Jews are prisoners in Babylon! What is to stop the Medes and the Persians from breaking into the city and killing everyone, Jews included?*

But he didn't have a chance to feel dejected for long. Suddenly there was a loud knocking at the gate. Caleb stared at Daniel. *What now?* he wondered.

Daniel opened the gate to find a detachment of palace guards staring him in the face. "Excuse us, sir," the captain of the guard stammered. "We apologize for disturbing you at this hour, but the king has commanded that you come to the banquet hall." He sounded frightened. His hands were shaking, and Caleb could see his face was as pale as the moon now rising rapidly in the eastern sky.

"Give me a moment. I'll be right with you," Daniel said respectfully and then turned to Uncle Jabez, Malik, and the boys. "You can wait here for me, if you want."

Caleb was really worried. *What does the king want with the old prophet at the palace? Is he in trouble?*

Suddenly, Caleb wanted to go with Daniel to the palace. He didn't know what he would do there or whether he would even be allowed inside, but he wanted to be there to stand with the old prophet. He didn't know where that kind of courage came from, and he was sure he didn't know what he was getting himself into, but he wanted to go anyway.

"They can come," the captain replied, seeing the look on Caleb's face. "But they've got to keep out of the way and not slow us down." His voice was shaking now too.

Daniel already had his sandals on and his evening tunic. "Come along, then," he said to Uncle Jabez, Malik, and the boys.

They hurried along the torch-lit pathways through the gardens and over a high walkway bridge that spanned the Euphrates River. The captain led the way, and his guards followed along behind the group.

As they crossed the bridge, Caleb stopped to stare down at the dark waters of the river. There was something unusual about the river, but he couldn't quite say what it was. But he didn't have time to consider such things for long and hurried to catch up with the others.

In a few minutes, they arrived at the banquet hall. As they entered the main gate to the palace, Caleb noticed something strange. Any guards that should have been on duty were strangely absent. *Where are all the guards? The ones at the gate are drunk, and there are none here at the palace either. What is going on?*

He had to hurry to catch up with the others as they entered the corridors of the palace. Floors of white marble glistened in the glow of torchlight. Statues and images stood in every corner and in little niches set in the walls. Long, silky curtains of blue, white, and purple blew gently in the night breeze.

There was gold everywhere. Caleb had never seen so much of it in his life. Decorative gold vases stood on long, narrow tables in the corridors. Golden candle sconces were mounted on the walls. Clasps of gold held the colorful curtains in long, arching loops.

The glitz and glitter of the palace overwhelmed Caleb, but he had a strange sensation about everything he was seeing. A sense of danger was in the air, as if something terrible was about to happen! He tried to shake the feeling, but it wouldn't go away.

Something else was wrong. The wild music he had heard all night had died away. In its place were screams and moans of people—hundreds of people. *Where is the sound coming from? Are people dying in the palace? Has the enemy already broken through the city walls and begun killing Babylonians?*

27

Caleb didn't have long to wonder. He and the others rounded a corner and entered a banquet room with a high ceiling where they got the shock of their lives. Tamzi fell back against Caleb, and Malik dropped to his knees. Uncle Jabez grabbed a nearby statue to steady himself. Even Daniel blinked hard at the terrifying sight before their eyes. Mysterious letters of fire were emblazoned across the white plaster of the palace wall, written it seemed, by some unseen force.

Caleb froze. This was the most frightening thing he had ever seen. He didn't know what to say! He didn't know what to do! He could only stand and stare at the fiery letters.

How did the letters get there? Were they written with a sooty torch? Were they carved into the wall and filled with burning pitch? Or did something else mysteriously make the letters?

Everyone in the banquet hall was staring at the frightening letters, too, but no one could read them. They seemed to be written in a code. If he hadn't known better, Caleb would have thought he was dreaming.

Caleb glanced around the banquet hall and realized he was in a room with the most important people in the kingdom. Plush couches of gold upholstered in purple velvet were everywhere in the huge vaulted room. Silver tables groaned with the weight of pastries and fruits and barbecued meats. Here and there servants stood with flasks of wine and platters loaded with all kinds of appetizers.

It was a picture worth a thousand words. Caleb's eyes saw it all in a sweep of the room, but none of it seemed to matter anymore to the guests gathered in the banquet hall. They were dressed in their best robes for the celebration, but now they had eyes for one thing only—the fiery handwriting on the wall. Advisers, generals, and government leaders, along with their wives, stared at the letters. Standing above them, by his throne on a dais, was King Belshazzar, dressed in his finest purple robes.

The king's face was as white as snow, and his hands and knees were shaking uncontrollably. Every few seconds he opened his mouth to say something, but no words would come.

"What happened here?" Caleb stammered as he grabbed Daniel's arm.

"Obviously something supernatural." Daniel took a step forward to get a better view through the crowd.

The captain of the palace guard came to stand by Daniel. "It was ghostly," he muttered. "Like nothing I've ever seen before! A hand appeared out of nowhere and began writing. A hand, I tell you, but it wasn't attached to anything. It was just there all by itself!" His voice shook as if this was the coldest night on earth. "I'll never forget it as long as I live!"

Everyone in the hall continued staring at the letters of fire, waiting it seemed for something else to happen.

Suddenly, a woman of regal bearing, standing on the dais by the king, spotted Daniel. "He's here," she gasped. "The holy man has arrived in whom the Spirit of the Living God reigns.

"Oh, king, live forever!" she called out to Belshazzar above the wailing and screaming in the banquet hall. "Don't be afraid! Daniel, whose name is Belteshazzar, has come as you requested. As you know, he served under your grandfather Nebuchadnezzar."

The king turned from the dreadful writing on the wall. His eyes were wide with fear. He seemed to be in a daze, as if in shock, and was unable to speak.

"The man you called for is here to help," the woman on the dais kept saying. "He has been gifted with a keen mind to interpret dreams, explain riddles, and solve difficult problems. That's why King Nebuchadnezzar appointed him as chief of the magicians, enchanters, astrologers, and diviners in his court.

"Don't worry, my lord," she added as she turned again to stare at the letters of fire on the wall. "Belteshazzar will tell you the meaning of the mysterious writing."

A look of terror was on the king's face, but he finally found his voice. "So you are Daniel"—he trembled—"one of the exiles King Nebuchadnezzar brought from Judah? I've heard about you, that the spirit of the gods is in you, and that you have outstanding wisdom.

"I brought all my advisers and astrologers here to read the writing and tell me what it means. I promised them rewards and promotions, a royal robe, and the golden chain of authority to help me rule the kingdom, but they couldn't solve it." King Belshazzar put his hands to his head, gave the blazing letters on the wall another look, and then regained his composure.

"Come!" he beckoned to Daniel with his outstretched hand, which was shaking almost as much as his voice. "I have heard that you are able to give interpretations and solve impossible predicaments. If you can read this writing and tell me what it means, you will be given a robe of purple to wear in my presence and a gold chain around your neck. I will make you the prime minister, and you shall become the third highest ruler in the kingdom of Babylon!"

Daniel brushed the promise of gifts aside. "You may keep your presents," he told the king respectfully. "Give your rewards to someone else. However, I will read the writing for you and tell you what it means."

The screaming and wailing in the banquet hall slowly died away as more and more people realized Daniel was talking to the king. Caleb was amazed at the transformation that came over the crowd of partiers. Everyone strained their necks to see the old prophet, and some had to stand on the tip of their toes to get a glimpse of him where he stood near the king. It was as if they were waiting to hear the very last words of hope on earth.

"Your Majesty, I count it an honor to stand before you and speak words from the Creator of heaven and earth," Daniel said. "It was He who gave your grandfather Nebuchadnezzar sovereignty, greatness, glory, and splendor over the empire of Babylon. Because of the high position my God gave your grandfather, all the nations and peoples of every language dreaded and feared him. If he wanted to humble his enemies, he did so.

If he wanted to execute them, he had the power to do that too. Those he wanted to promote were promoted.

"However, when his heart became arrogant and hardened with pride, he was removed from his throne and stripped of his dignity. He was driven away from people and given the mind of a beast. He lived with wild donkeys and ate grass like oxen. His body was wet with dew each night. For seven long years, he suffered until he was ready to admit that the Most High God is Sovereign over all kingdoms of the earth."

The king stared at Daniel, and his eyes grew more afraid by the moment. It was as if he knew what was coming next.

"But you, Belshazzar, grandson of the great Nebuchadnezzar, have not humbled yourself, though you knew all of this. Instead you have grown wicked, wanting only the pleasures of the world. You have praised the gods of silver and gold, of bronze, iron, wood, and stone, which cannot see or hear or understand. You have blasphemed the Lord of heaven by using the cups and goblets from His holy temple. You have drunk wine from them, you and your nobles, your wives and your concubines. Sadly, you have not honored the God who holds your life in His hand and records your every deed in the books of heaven. For these reasons, He sent the hand that wrote the inscription."

Caleb was horrified to see that everyone in the giant banquet hall was indeed drinking from Jehovah's holy vessels. The golden goblets and silver cups from Judah's ancient temple had been brought here by the palace steward, just as Malik had said. It turned Caleb's stomach to see the vessels desecrated like this. Some were still in the hands of the partiers, with red wine dripping from them. However, many had fallen to the floor, dropped by the hands of those now staring at the glowing letters on the wall. He wanted to stoop and pick the cups and goblets up but was afraid to touch them where they lay. They were sacred; they were God's vessels; and they were to be used only by the priests of the Lord in His temple!

How can these pagan partiers treat God's holy vessels like this? he wondered in amazement. *How can they defile the sacred vessels that were meant for the worship of Jehovah only, the Sovereign of the universe?*

Daniel is right, Caleb thought. A mysterious, supernatural hand had been sent to tell King Belshazzar he was a vain man. He was proud, selfish, evil, and cruel. Because of this, bad things were going to happen. There was no other way, it seemed. The handwriting was on the wall.

28

Daniel stood unafraid in the banquet hall. Caleb had to admire the old prophet.

The prophet never took his eyes from King Belshazzar, who was hanging his head in shame. "And now, Your Majesty, this is the inscription written on the wall: MENE, MENE, TEKEL, UPHARSIN." Daniel's eyes were blazing like the words on the wall. "Here is what the words mean. MENE: God has numbered the days of your reign and brought it to an end.

"TEKEL: You have been weighed on the scales and haven't measured up.

"UPHARSIN: You had your chance on the throne, Your Majesty, but your time is up!" Daniel's voice rose to a crescendo. "You're finished. Your kingdom is divided and given to the Medes and the Persians!"

King Belshazzar stared at Daniel blankly, as though he hadn't heard the death sentence. "Bring my best purple robe here and the golden chain," he finally ordered with a hollow, emotionless voice. "This man deserves the best gifts in the land!"

The king's attendants rushed forward with the rewards fit for a king: a purple satin robe; an official signet ring; and an exquisite golden chain with miniature lions, bulls, and dragons carved into it.

Daniel waved the gifts off as he pointed to heaven. "It's over, King Belshazzar. Tonight your soul will be required of you!"

Caleb was astonished at the sight before him. A look of panic gripped the king's face once again, and his voice rose on the night air as he began to wail pitifully. But there was nothing anyone could do. The final day of judgment had come for King Belshazzar and his subjects. God had predicted it, and the old prophet had been His messenger. This very night Babylon would fall into the hands of the Medes and the Persians. Daniel had said it, and Caleb was now sure of it.

At that very moment, there was a cry of alarm outside the banquet hall. "Run for your lives!" someone screamed. "The enemy has invaded the city!"

It was now Caleb's turn to panic. His eyes darted frantically this way and that. *Enemy soldiers are in the city! The Medes and the Persians must have invaded Babylon!*

"Come on," Uncle Jabez shouted as he grabbed Caleb's arm and pushed him toward the corridor to the palace entrance. "We've got to get out of here."

Malik and Tamzi turned to follow them, but Daniel halted everyone in their tracks. "Don't go that way," he commanded. "I've got a better idea. This way!" he said with a jerk of his head.

Caleb and Tamzi scurried after him, but it wasn't hard to keep up. Daniel was an old man and unable to run like the rest of them. Yet it was surprising how quickly he moved, mostly because he knew exactly where he was going.

He led the way, taking them down a back corridor to a stairwell that descended into a lower level of the palace. Malik and Uncle Jabez took up the rear, along with Daniel's two attendants, keeping an eye out for any danger that might be coming from behind.

From there, they walked along narrow corridors where sooty torches dimly lit the way. Several times they heard screams above and behind them and had to duck into the shadows to hide. Then off they would go again until they finally emerged at the western edge of the palace into the lush gardens, which were damp with dew.

They silently crept along in the shadows among flowering plants and exotic greenery. Fountains tinkled in the tiled courtyards they passed, and crickets chirped in the darkness. The moon was riding high above the streets of Babylon, but Caleb didn't notice it. He could hear people running and screaming in the streets ahead of them. People were dying. It seemed that chaos and pandemonium were taking over the city. Swords clashed and spears clanked as they fell to the clay streets. Enemy horses clattered through gateways and back and forth across river bridges.

At one point, Daniel held up his hand to block their way before crossing a pathway. He was just in time because down the pathway raced several Babylonian soldiers! Persian mercenaries came behind them in hot pursuit, while yelling and bloodcurdling screams filled the air.

Everyone caught their breath at the narrow escape. When the way was clear, they hurried across and into the shadows again. They had several more close encounters before they finally found themselves in the tiled walkway leading to Daniel's apartment complex. What a relief it was to be back in familiar territory.

As they entered Daniel's suite of rooms, the prophet and his two servants quickly put out all the torches and closed the shuttered windows. The attendants brought everyone cool cups of water to drink and some flatbread and cheese.

"I think it would be good for you to stay with me tonight," Daniel said as they sat down to catch their breath. "The streets won't be safe until daybreak. By morning light, we'll have a better idea of what to expect."

"We can't stay," Malik protested as a dusty trickle of sweat ran down his face. "I've got to go home to my wife and daughter. We don't even know what's become of them."

"I know you're worried about them, but honestly, you'd better stay." Daniel put a hand on Malik's shoulder. "You and Jabez can't afford the risk. If you're on the streets tonight, the enemy may mistake you for Babylonian soldiers. As far as your families are concerned, they'll be safe, too, as long as they stay indoors. Cyrus has no thirst for blood. He just wants Babylon to surrender."

Malik didn't look so sure, but Uncle Jabez finally nodded. "He's right, Malik. Our wives would be very upset if they knew we were in danger on the streets tonight. I'm sure they would agree with Daniel."

"Jehovah will keep your families safe tonight. ' "There is no one like the God of [Israel]," ' Daniel began quoting a promise from the Scriptures.

" ' "Who rides the heavens to help you,
And in His excellency on the clouds.
The eternal God is your refuge,
And underneath are the everlasting arms" ' " (Deuteronomy 33:26, 27).

Sleeping mats were brought out for everyone, and they laid down to rest. It would be several hours yet before dawn crossed into the eastern sky.

Caleb tried to go to sleep; but it was difficult, even though he knew he should be tired. He was so keyed up that he couldn't relax. *What will happen in the morning? Will there be a battle in the streets of Babylon? Will people be caught and tortured? Will lots and lots of people die, or will the leaders of Babylon surrender? King Belshazzar wasn't willing to do that, but his wild parties didn't stop the enemy from invading Babylon. There seems to be little choice now.*

For a moment, Caleb had a thought of the king. *What has become of him and the wise men and advisers in the palace and the royal lady who had called Daniel to help the king?* Caleb tossed and turned as his weary thoughts and worries tumbled over one another. Fortunately, he drifted off to sleep sometime before dawn.

At the first light of dawn, Caleb was awake again when messengers arrived to give Daniel the latest news. Details of the enemy invasion and mysterious handwriting on the palace wall were beginning to come together.

"They diverted the Euphrates River," the messenger said as he knelt according to custom and bowed respectfully to Daniel. "Their army engineers wanted the water in the river to drop. That's why they dug a canal to channel the water out of the riverbed. That's how the enemy soldiers got into the city—they marched up the shallow riverbed, under the city wall, and through the river gates."

"How did they get through the gates?" Daniel inquired.

"Drunken guards left the gates untended. Some were left unbarred or slightly ajar. Others were wide open."

29

Caleb now knew that his impression of the night before had been real and wasn't just imagined. When they had arrived at the gates of the palace grounds, it seemed there wasn't a guard in sight. It must have been true. They must have been off attending parties, and the guards who were around were drunker than drunk. That's why Caleb, Tamzi, and the others had been able to go straight to Daniel's apartment suite.

"The struggle was over before it even got started," the messenger said. "Babylon never had a chance. The Medes and the Persians overtook the city with only a few minor skirmishes. Our soldiers didn't even put up a fight, and most of the guards in the towers were either drunk or sleeping."

Daniel nodded at each new detail.

"There's more," added the messenger. "When the Persian warriors stormed the palace, everyone had fled, except King Belshazzar and his royal guard who took refuge in the king's private chambers. His bodyguard tried to defend him, but it was pointless, and they were slaughtered— every one of them.

"The king himself was executed just before dawn," the messenger continued. "Belshazzar refused to surrender, claiming the gods of Babylon would protect him. 'You can't touch me!' he screamed at the Persian general who finally ordered his death. 'I've sacrificed to Marduk and arranged for every talisman and good-luck charm possible. He will save me!' "

"But he died at the hands of the Persian general anyway, didn't he?" Daniel asked solemnly. Caleb wondered that Daniel knew such a thing already, but then realized he shouldn't be surprised. The old prophet had talked with angels. He would know anything God wanted him to know.

The messenger hesitated for only a moment. "Yes, Your Honor," was all he would say.

The news was shocking but not surprising to Caleb. *Didn't Daniel predict this? Didn't the mysterious hand from heaven write King Belshazzar's epitaph on the wall of the palace?*

Caleb and Uncle Jabez hurried home. The sky was still a deep blue but slowly turning pink and a lighter shade of azure. Songbirds flitted from hanging vines to trees to rooftops in the dim light of dawn. Hummingbirds buzzed from flower to flower. Lizards climbed the walls of patios and gardens. Soon the sun would be peeking its way up over the eastern wall.

The streets were unusually quiet. *Where is everyone?* Caleb wondered. *Where is the enemy that has invaded the city?* As they crossed the bridge over the Euphrates, Caleb could see that the water level in the riverbed was indeed low—low enough to allow men to walk in it knee-deep, as the enemy soldiers must have done the night before.

They arrived home and found Aunt Helah sick with worry after staying awake all night. "Why didn't you come home?" she wailed, more upset than Caleb ever remembered seeing her.

"We wanted to come," Uncle Jabez tried to comfort her, "but Daniel warned us it would be very dangerous. He said we'd likely be struck down if we were found sneaking through the streets!"

"Well, you could have sent word or something." Aunt Helah's eyes were blazing like fire as she angrily pounded some barley in a grinding mortar.

"And if we had done that, the messenger might have been spotted and killed."

Grandpa Obed kept shaking his head. "I tried to calm her nerves," he said, "but I wasn't successful. When a woman's mind is made up, there's not much a man can do, I guess."

Uncle Jabez gave his wife an affectionate hug. "There's nothing better than having a loving mother and wife at home who is worried about us. We just couldn't help it last night, Helah, that's all."

They ate a warm breakfast of barley porridge and *leben*, and Caleb almost forgot that the Medes and the Persians had invaded the city. Everything seemed so peaceful in the family courtyard as they sat down to eat, but that didn't last long.

Before breakfast was over, Tamzi was at the gate. "King Cyrus is getting ready to enter the city gates," he shouted excitedly. "Everybody's excited! Some people are scared, but they say he's coming peacefully."

Caleb jumped to his feet. "How did you get here?" he asked in surprise. "I thought it was too dangerous to be out on the streets."

Tamzi shrugged. "Not anymore."

"What about the enemy soldiers? They're not killing people?"

"Nope. A few Babylonian soldiers died last night when they put up a fight, but the Medo-Persian solders are treating everybody pretty well now."

"Wow!" Caleb picked up his bowl and gulped down the rest of his porridge. "Can I go with Tamzi?" he asked Uncle Jabez.

"I'll go with you," Uncle Jabez got up, too, and went to put on a clean tunic. "You'd better put something else on too," he told Caleb with a peculiar smile. "You're a sight! We can't afford to look undignified if we're supposed to welcome the conquering king."

It was an exciting morning after all that had happened the night before. Everyone in the family went to see King Cyrus's military parade as he entered the city through the Ishtar Gate. And it was quite an entrance.

There was standing room only on the streets. To get a better view, Caleb and his family climbed up the inner staircase to the wall above the Ishtar Gate. When they arrived near Isi's watchtower, they found Tamzi and his family there ahead of them, already cheering.

The wide promenade below was lined with thousands and thousands of Babylonian citizens all dressed in their best. "This is the craziest thing I've ever seen," Caleb had to shout above the noise of the crowds. "We're not being dragged before our captors to be tortured or killed. Instead, we're welcoming them, as if they're our own conquering champions coming home."

"This is a strange turn of events," Uncle Jabez acknowledged, "but you have to admit, very few of the commoners in Babylon ever liked King Belshazzar. He was a cruel bully and a vain and pompous man."

The parade was sensational—a celebration, it seemed, to end all celebrations. Down the broad avenue, the parade marched with King Cyrus the conqueror at its head. He was dressed in his military uniform and armor, and what a grand sight he was! In his chariot attended by a driver and archer, he stood handsomely under a colorful umbrella canopy. Two prancing white horses with decorative chest armor and braided manes pulled the chariot on its wheels of decorative gold.

The crowd cheered madly when Cyrus first entered the city gate, and as he passed, their enthusiastic welcome grew louder and louder. "Hail to the king!" thousands shouted. "Long live our monarch, the liberator of our people!" others screamed. Some even ran out into the promenade to greet him and throw him kisses with wild emotion.

"This is incredible!" Caleb shouted above the roar of the crowd. "I never would have believed it if I hadn't seen it with my own eyes! I guess people really were fed up with things here in Babylon."

Behind Cyrus came his three generals dressed in their finest military gear, riding horses fit for kings. Next rode the lesser military officers, and after them on foot, thousands of soldiers, both Medes and Persians.

On and on the procession paraded up the promenade to the palace—chariots and horsemen, archers and footmen, artillery and wagons full of war trophies from Sippar. The crowds continued to cheer the whole morning until the last of the procession had marched by.

With the Medes and the Persians in control of Babylon, Caleb realized a new day had dawned for the Jews. The destruction of Babylon, which everyone had feared, did not take place. King Cyrus turned out to be a wise and intelligent ruler. Under his strong leadership, things returned to normal. Business in the marketplace started to pick up. The Jews continued to make plans for the future.

"People say Cyrus is famous for letting conquered nations keep their places of worship, and that's a good sign for us," Uncle Jabez said one evening as they were sitting down to supper. "If this is so, it seems

Jeremiah's prediction about our return to Judah has a much better chance of coming true than we thought."

Caleb's eyes lit up at his uncle's comments. "That makes sense." He took another sip of his lentil stew. "Daniel said the same thing. He told us Cyrus would show favor to the Jews here in Babylon and maybe even set us free. Do you think it's actually going to happen now?"

Uncle Jabez smiled. "I don't know. Let's ask the prophet when we see him next."

30

Caleb and his family met for worship at the synagogue the following Sabbath, and Daniel smiled when he heard Caleb's eager question. "Yes, I definitely think it will happen," he said, but then his face grew serious. "King Cyrus will be the one to write a decree that lets us go, but it's not going to be as easy as we might think. I've been shown the prince of darkness will work to prevent the decree from being written."

Caleb's face grew troubled too. "You mean Lucifer? The evil one fallen from heaven?" he asked.

Daniel nodded. "Exactly. The Lord's promises for His chosen people will be much easier to fulfill if we go back to Judah. The Anointed One must come to save us from our sins, and it should not have to happen in the land of our captivity."

"And you believe the evil one will try to get in the way?" Caleb stared at Daniel.

"He'll try, but let me make something very clear," Daniel reassured Caleb. "God always wins. Satan can't hold out forever, and neither will King Cyrus."

Daniel was right. Cyrus did write the decree, with a little encouragement from the Jewish elders in Babylon. Zaccai and Daniel brought the writings of Isaiah to the Persian king and showed him the famous prophecy where he was mentioned by name, nearly one hundred and fifty years before.

"Thus says the LORD to His anointed,
To Cyrus, whose right hand I have held—
To subdue nations before him
And loose the armor of kings,
To open before him the double doors,
So that the gates will not be shut" (Isaiah 45:1).

" 'He is My shepherd,
And he shall perform all My pleasure,
Saying to Jerusalem, "You shall be built,"
And to the temple, "Your foundation shall be laid" ' " (Isaiah 44:28).

Cyrus was astonished that the God of heaven would write a special message for him before he was even born. He was so impressed, in fact, that he finally issued a public proclamation allowing the Jews to return to their homeland:

Thus says Cyrus king of Persia:
All the kingdoms of the earth the LORD God of heaven has given me. And He has commanded me to build Him a house at Jerusalem which is in Judah. Who is among you of all His people? May his God be with him, and let him go up to Jerusalem which is in Judah, and build the house of the LORD God of Israel (Ezra 1:2, 3).

There was great rejoicing in the streets of the Jewish settlement where Caleb lived when the royal crier read the proclamation. "Finally, God's promises are being fulfilled for our people," Uncle Jabez said, and Caleb noticed a tear steal its way down his cheek.

"Well, Grandpa, I guess you were wrong," Caleb said. "You said you'd die here, but God knew better. He knew you needed to go home to the land of your fathers." Grandpa didn't say anything, but Caleb saw him swallow hard and noticed tears on his face too.

King Cyrus also commanded his officials to release the sacred Jewish vessels of gold and silver taken from Jerusalem. Malik was very excited when he found out. He and Tamzi went to share the good news with Caleb and his family right away.

"They've turned over all the treasures from Judah's temple," he said excitedly. "Get this! We have more than five thousand sacred vessels in all. You can take them back with you when you go—platters and basins and knives and urns, all made of gold and silver."

"What about the golden goblets and silver cups used at the king's big banquet?" Caleb asked. "What happened to them?"

"I have them too." Malik gave Caleb a wink. "They were put back in my care when Cyrus wrote the decree. It took me several days to sort them out in the storeroom where they were kept since the night of the invasion. I have them in custody now."

Caleb was excited beyond words. To be able to go home to the land of Judah had been his biggest dream for the longest time. He was disappointed, however, to find that not everyone shared the same enthusiasm.

Many Jews decided not to make the long journey southwest to the land of their fathers. They had been in Babylon for so long that they were used to it. They had their businesses and homes, and many, contrary to the commands of God, had even married Babylonians.

But Caleb and his family were going. There was no hesitation on their part. Returning to Judah was the most important thing to them, and they wouldn't have it any other way.

And wonder of wonders, Tamzi's family decided to go too. "We aren't Jews, but we want to worship the Living God," Malik told Uncle Jabez one Sabbath as they joined Caleb's family at the synagogue. "We've given it a lot of thought, and we think living among the Jews is the best way to do that. We've learned so much about Jehovah from your family, and we've come to love Him as our Creator too."

After the midday meal, the boys ran down to the river to see if they could find Allamu and tell him the good news. "We're going back to the land of Judah," Tamzi crowed when they found the blind beggar sitting under his usual palm tree. "King Cyrus wrote a decree to let all the Jews go home, and Caleb's family has invited us to go with them."

"I'll miss you, boys." Allamu's face dropped at the news. "You've been kind to me."

A smile slowly began to form on Caleb's face. "Are you thinking what I'm thinking?" He grinned at Tamzi.

Tamzi squinted. "Yeah, but do you really think it'll work?"

Caleb jumped to his feet, "Come on! Let's ask our fathers before we say more."

The boys raced home to share the idea with their families. "We think Allamu should go back to Judah with us," Caleb told his uncle. "He has no family, and he's told us so many stories about our people. It's like he's already one of us. I know he'd be happy among our people, because he believes in the power of our God."

Uncle Jabez looked doubtful. "He's blind. How would we get him there?"

"He could ride in the donkey cart on our baggage."

"And where would he stay when we got to Judah?"

"He could stay with us." Caleb was really getting excited. "He can help us in our pottery shop. He's not a lot different from Grandpa. We could probably teach him how to make jars and pots too, don't you think?"

"Really?" Uncle Jabez was impressed by Caleb's kindness and compassion. He turned to Aunt Helah. "What do you think? Shall we give it a try?"

"Why not?" Aunt Helah smiled. "Allamu's got no one else. We could become his family, and it might be a way to save him for the kingdom of God."

The next morning the boys went to visit Daniel at his apartment. "There's only a few more weeks before everyone leaves for Judah," Tamzi said excitedly, "and we were wondering if you're going to go with us."

"Yeah, I want to see the look on your face when you see your homeland," Caleb said. "You weren't much older than us when you left, were you?"

"That's right." Daniel smiled at the boys' enthusiasm but then grew silent.

"So what do you think?" Tamzi asked impatiently.

Daniel bowed his head. "I would love to go with you and your families," he sighed. "There's nothing I would like more."

"OK!" Tamzi's face grew even more excited. "Then let's start getting you packed!"

31

Caleb read much in Daniel's sad eyes, and he guessed what was on the old prophet's mind. "You think you're too old to make the trip, don't you?" he asked hesitantly.

"That's right," Daniel nodded a bit sheepishly.

"But Allamu's going to go," Tamzi protested, "And he's old."

"Yes, but my situation is different. I have much to do here in Babylon for the new Medo-Persian government. They're asking me to do more and more in the palace. And," Daniel's voice trailed off.

"And what?" Tamzi pressed the point.

"And God has told me that it's His plan for me to stay in Babylon." The prophet's head dropped. "I'll not be going with you to Judah."

There was a long moment of silence. Caleb didn't know what to say. It sounded so final.

"Will you give us a blessing then, before we go?" Caleb finally asked the old prophet.

"Of course." Daniel gave the boys a courageous smile and then drew the boys close to lay a hand on each head. "You will be grown men in just a few years, and when that time comes, remember these words," he said. "Keep them in your heart for as long as you live.

> "Blessed is the man
> Who walks not in the counsel of the ungodly,
> Nor stands in the path of sinners,
> Nor sits in the seat of the scornful;
> But his delight is in the law of the LORD,
> And in His law he meditates day and night.
> He shall be like a tree
> Planted by the rivers of water,
> That brings forth its fruit in its season,
> Whose leaf also shall not wither;
> And whatever he does shall prosper" (Psalm 1:1–3).

The boys left Daniel with their spirits low, but they couldn't stay down for long. "We're going to the Promised Land!" Caleb shouted as they raced off down the street toward home. *Yee-haw!*

Caleb's family packed and repacked their belongings over the next few days. There wasn't much room in the donkey cart, but clothes, bedding, and food needed to go. And, of course, there were the tools from the family pottery shop: the pottery wheels, the iron door to the kiln, and the wooden trough for treading clay.

Uncle Jabez sold the house to another Jewish family and bought another cart and donkey with some of the money. He also bought two camels.

"We can't leave here empty-handed," he said. "If we can take most of our belongings with us, we'll have a much easier time starting over in Judah."

But there was more excitement to come. "Guess what!" Saarah said one evening when the family gathered for a meal in the courtyard. "Jemi and her family are going back to Judah with us!"

"No kidding!" Caleb's jaw dropped in surprise, and his heart skipped a beat. "I thought her family wasn't very religious."

"They aren't"—Saarah winked at Caleb—"but her father said he had a dream. An angel told him they should go back to the land of our ancestors. When he talked to Zaccai about it, the scribe told him he'd better obey the angel. Zaccai said he thought God was probably trying to warn

Jemi's father about bad days to come for Jews in Babylon."

"Really?" Caleb could hardly believe his ears. He didn't know what to think, but he had to admit he liked Jemi. She was a sweet girl and pretty besides. The fact that she and her family wanted to obey God was really good news. That was the kind of girl he knew he could one day learn to like a lot. *Who knows? Maybe even some day . . .* but that was as far as Caleb got in his thoughts because Tamzi was at the gate once again.

"Come on, Caleb!" he shouted. "My father wants help at the warehouse packing all the gold and silver vessels for Judah. We've got lots to do. He wants to wrap each and every sacred artifact in linen cloth and repack them in crates."

Caleb jumped up from the meal. "How are we going to transport all the artifacts?" he asked. "They're so heavy."

Tamzi shrugged. "I guess King Cyrus has given us money from his treasury to buy donkeys, oxen, and wagons to haul everything."

"Really?" Caleb grinned. "Wow! That's going to be a lot of wagons!" And his prediction turned out to be true. By the time everything was packed, a total of forty wagons had been loaded with all the crates of sacred vessels.

Caleb was very excited about the coming trip. He could hardly sleep each night as the day approached for them to leave. He loved their home in Babylon with its big family courtyard. He loved the rooftop where he and Tamzi had spent so many nights telling stories and counting stars. He even had to admit he'd miss the family pottery shop where he had helped to provide a living for the family. But he liked the idea of making the trip to the land of Judah too. Ancient Jerusalem had so many wonderful stories in its past, and even if the walls and gates were down, they could be rebuilt. Caleb was sure Judah could return once again to its days of glory.

There were also the sacred vessels King Cyrus had returned to the Jewish leaders. The gold and silver things from Solomon's glorious temple were going home to Judah, and in Caleb's mind, nothing would bring them better luck.

Of course, he knew it was Jehovah's blessings that would return them to Judah and bring them prosperity in the land of their fathers—not luck. When it came to the worship of the one true God, there was no such thing as good luck.

The day Caleb's people left Babylon to go home to the old country was the biggest moment of his life. But it wasn't as big as the day he had discovered the temple treasures in the royal archives of Babylon. What a day that had been, and now those holy vessels, stolen so long ago, were returning home to Judah with the Jews once again!

God had blessed His people beyond their wildest hopes! Caleb knew life would never be the same for him or any of the others leaving for Judah. "And that's the way it should be," he said to himself, as he and Tamzi raced out through the Ishtar Gate to join the caravan of Jewish travelers heading west.